"I told you no article."

"You said no interview. I make the decisions about what to print in this newspaper. And I decided to publish the article anyway."

"You had no right."

"Yes, I did. Freedom of the press is protected by the US Constitution."

Laurel sounded so stiff and pompous, Yates almost laughed. But he didn't. He was too fired up. Fact was, he hadn't been this stirred up in so long, he'd forgotten how it felt.

He leaned in until they were nose to nose.

"What about my right to privacy?"

Laurel held her ground. She was no coward. It was one of the things he'd admired about her. She'd always wanted to go public with their relationship, to show their families that Kenos and Trudeaus didn't have to be enemies.

He didn't want to remember that now. Thinking about their past brought back memories he'd rather forget. Memories of a generous, loving, really smart woman whom he'd liked too much.

But when she learned his secret, would she be willing to risk an uncertain future?

Linda Goodnight, a *New York Times* bestselling author and winner of a RITA® Award in inspirational fiction, has appeared on the Christian bestseller list. Her novels have been translated into more than a dozen languages. Active in orphan ministry, Linda enjoys writing fiction that carries a message of hope in a sometimes dark world. She and her husband live in Oklahoma. Visit her website, lindagoodnight.com, for more information.

Visit the Author Profile page at LoveInspired.com for more titles.

The Cowboy's Journey Home

Linda Goodnight

LOVE INSPIRED
INSPIRATIONAL ROMANCE

LOVE INSPIRED®
INSPIRATIONAL ROMANCE

Recycling programs for this product may not exist in your area.

ISBN-13: 978-1-335-58514-1

The Cowboy's Journey Home

Copyright © 2022 by Linda Goodnight

Love Inspired
22 Adelaide St. West, 41st Floor
Toronto, Ontario M5H 4E3, Canada
www.LoveInspired.com

Printed in U.S.A.

For I the Lord thy God will hold thy right hand,
saying unto thee, Fear not; I will help thee.
—*Isaiah* 41:13

In memory of Travis,
and in praise of Jesus Messiah.

Chapter One

The jig is up. We know you're in there. You might as well come out.

Yates Trudeau stared at the text from his brother and released a word his mother would have washed his mouth out for saying.

The Belgian Malinois sitting on the grass at his side lifted his regal head in question. Quietly alert, the dog kept watchful eyes on his new handler, awaiting command.

"Position compromised," Yates said softly as he slid the cell phone back into his camo jacket and buttoned the pocket. "No fish for us today."

After reclaiming his rod and reel, he slowly turned the handle to bring in the spinner bait while he debated this unexpected turn of events.

Hidden Pond, as the Trudeau family had dubbed this wilderness water hole, was pristine today. Glassy calm beneath the overcast sky—perfect for snagging a bass or two.

The weather remained chilly, but the clean air held hints that spring was right around the corner. Pleasant days like this, after a long winter, got him up and moving, though his movements were not as fast or as precise as they'd once been.

He and his dog had been enjoying themselves in this tranquil, empty wilderness. Until the text.

Justice, too well disciplined to muddy the waters, had

alternately perched on the grass at his side or romped through the tall dry weeds, disappearing occasionally into the underbrush. For once in his life, the MWD—or military working dog, to civilians—wasn't ferreting out the bad guys. He was having fun.

This was only the second time since becoming a recon scout that Yates's whereabouts had been detected. The first had ended his military career. Fortunately no one was shooting at him today. These weren't enemy combatants. This was his brother Wade and his cousin Bowie, who was as near to being a brother as a man could be.

And Yates wasn't hiding. Not at all. He was healing.

He dropped a hand to the dog's upright, attentive ears, pondering his next move.

"What do you think, Justice?"

The Malinois turned golden eyes his way as if to say, "Time to go."

Yates nodded. "Roger that."

He'd planned to reveal himself in his own time, in his own way, when he was able to walk into the ranch house without so much as a limp or a grimace. He had wanted to appear hale and hearty again, not the pale, skinny creature the army had released a few months ago. A man had his pride. And Yates Trudeau had more than his share.

So no, he wasn't hiding from anyone. He was doing things his own way.

If he'd really been hiding, they would never have spotted him. A recon scout didn't survive long in terrorist pods around the world otherwise. He'd noticed Bowie's hidden cameras weeks ago, though he'd hoped no one would recognize him just yet.

He wasn't suffering from PTSD. He didn't hate the world or the military. In fact, he'd loved his job, liked the military brotherhood. He'd enjoyed his lifestyle, had even dated now and then when he wasn't on assignment, concealed in some dangerous spot with binoculars to his face.

Now he was just tired and at loose ends.

He'd had the rest of his life all planned out. Now he didn't.

Like Jinx, the reclusive old vet who lived on a nearby hill, Yates had needed to be alone for a while. Alone to sort out what he'd do with the rest of his life. Alone to let his body heal—to hope it would.

Ah, well. His timetable was pushed up a bit. Adapt and assimilate.

He tossed his loose fishing tackle into the metal box and snicked it closed with the same stealth that he did everything. A soldier could get killed fast if he was noisy.

Picking up the box and shouldering his rod and reel and rifle, he turned to gaze toward the ranch. He couldn't see it from here, but he could feel it.

With a silent hand signal to Justice, he began trudging through the thick pine-and-hickory forest surrounding Hidden Pond.

During the months in rehab when he'd been especially low, thoughts of Sundown Ranch had kept him sane. Going to the home where he'd grown into a man promised both pleasure and pain. Pleasure to see Wade and Bowie and his horses. Pain at the emptiness, the loss, the grief he'd left at Sundown Ranch. It would still be there because his parents and baby brother wouldn't be.

He couldn't have saved his parents. Fourteen-year-old Trent was a different matter.

Painfully aware that hurrying too much and stepping in a hole could prove disastrous to his damaged body, he paused to survey the terrain in front of him.

To dispel the melancholy that threatened any time he remembered his little brother, which was pretty much every single day, he pressed a hand against the rough trunk of a tall Ponderosa pine. Pressed until it hurt. Sticky sap stuck to his palm along with a few bits of splintery bark. He wiped the hand on his camo pants, inhaled the pungent scent.

Wade thought Yates blamed him for Trent's death. Maybe he had at first, a deflection for his own guilt. But Wade didn't know all the facts about that day.

Yates looked up into the gunmetal-gray sky. A noisy flock of blackbirds passed overhead, their combined wing-beats like distant clapping.

How would he be greeted? With joy? Anger? A million questions? Probably all three.

Yates started hiking again. He'd left his truck five klicks down the hill, beneath a stand of pines near an old, abandoned hunters' cabin. He'd stayed there a few times to hunt and fish whenever weather allowed, but mostly he lived in his RV in Centerville. Far enough away from the town of Sundown Valley to remain incognito, close enough to feel home. He couldn't deny the yearning for these woods and the familiar smells and sights. For family.

The dog heard the woman and kids before Yates did. Justice nudged his dangling hand, a soft whine issuing between canine lips. *Friendlies*, he seemed to say.

Yates was in no mood for company. Not yet. Not until he processed the homecoming he'd put off for years.

Silently, he slid into a stand of thick, tangled brush. *Blackberry vines.*

Yates allowed a wry smile. Of course he'd choose berry bushes. They had thorns. One dug into his thigh. He ignored it, could ignore pain for hours. What was a little thorn in the flesh to a well-trained soldier?

And wasn't there a scripture verse that mentioned something about thorns in the flesh? Not that he'd opened a Bible in a while. A very long while.

He was distracted from thoughts of his abandoned faith

when a small girl, maybe four or five, frolicked into view in the grassy clearing between the crowded stands of evergreen trees. A dark-skinned cutie with a giant red bow in her brown hair, she sang at the top of her lungs.

"Megan, stop yelling. You'll scare away the wildlife."

A slightly older and clearly wiser girl appeared from the evergreens. She, too, was dark of hair and skin but wore thick, purple-framed glasses and a cowgirl hat, also purple.

"I'm singing to Jesus." Megan pointed a tiny finger toward the sky. "He likes it."

"What if a bear hears you and eats us?"

Megan stopped singing, her eyes widening.

Three more children came into sight, followed by a slender woman in shiny waterproof sports pants and a snug windbreaker, with a messy, honey-colored mass of hair on top of her head. The way she tromped through the woods, she made enough noise in her practical hiking boots and swish-swish pants to ward off every bear within a hundred miles.

"Chelsey, don't frighten her." To the little one, the woman said, "Megan, singing is a great way to scare away bears. Let's all sing. God likes it."

In a charming, if slightly off-key, collaboration of voices, the little party joined a now-smiling Megan in a round of "He's Got the Whole World in His Hands."

Yates remembered singing that song in vacation Bible school as a kid. Back then, he'd been comforted by the thought that God was holding him in the palm of His hand, no matter what happened. That was the trouble with being a kid. The bad things came later, and since then, he'd not felt in tune with God at all. Even less now that his career was over and he faced an uncertain future.

The singing ended, and the woman shrugged out of a backpack and began unloading picnic supplies.

Great. He was stuck in a thorny blackberry bush, and they were settling in for the afternoon.

Something about his unwanted adult guest seemed familiar, but with these massive bushes in his line of sight, he didn't have a clear look at her face. He had once known everyone in and around Sundown Valley.

The two older girls, maybe seven or eight—though he was no judge of kids—helped her spread a tablecloth. Then the five girls and one slender woman plopped down.

As she handed around sandwiches, the woman began to talk about Jesus being the creator of the universe.

"According to the book of John, 'All things were made by Him, and without Him was not any thing made that was made.'" She laughed lightly at the end of the tongue-twisting scripture. Hers was a lilting laugh, warm and pleasant. And also familiar.

Something nudged at the back of his brain, though he couldn't quite pull the memory forward.

"You mean Jesus made these sandwiches?" The older girl she'd called Chelsey lifted the top slice of wheat bread and gazed beneath as if expecting to see Jesus waving at her.

The thought amused him. In fact, the whole scene amused him.

The woman laughed again—that sunny, sweet sound that lit up the clearing. "He made the animals and plants that eventually became this sandwich. And the people who put it all together."

"Cool. I'm eating a Jesus sandwich." Chelsey took a big, exaggerated chomp.

Yates pressed his lips together to keep from laughing out loud.

For years, he'd been a silent observer, watching people's movements, but suddenly he felt like a voyeur, as if he shouldn't be here, though this was his property. They were the trespassers.

Still, he should make his presence known before one of the little girls accidentally stumbled upon him and he scared the dickens out of her.

But watching the exchange and listening to innocent childish chatter was pure enjoyment. Except the sandwiches made him hungry. When was the last time he'd actually felt hungry?

One of the other children, not to be outdone by Chelsey, pulled up a handful of grass. "Jesus made this grass too."

"Yes. Look around, girls. Everything you see in nature was made by God's creative genius. Plants and animals and clouds and all the colors."

"Even different colors of people?" Megan looked at her tawny-brown arm.

"Absolutely." The woman hooked an elbow around the girl's shoulders and gave her a side hug. "All the different shades of people are like colorful flowers in God's perfect garden. The world would be so dull without them."

"Does God laugh?" Chelsey, the thinker, asked.

The messy bun wiggled as the woman nodded. "*We* laugh, don't we? And we're made in His image. So yes, I think He laughs a lot. He's probably smiling right now at five little girls who love Him and are outside enjoying the world He created."

A frown creased Chelsey's brow. "What's an 'image,' Miss Laurel?"

Miss Laurel?

The name stunned Yates. He only knew one woman named Laurel.

Laurel Maxwell?

Under cover of the continuing conversation, Yates shifted his position the slightest bit to enable a clearer view.

Sure enough. Ten feet away sat the woman he'd left

behind, a woman he should never have been romantically involved with.

A woman who had every reason to despise him—and probably did.

Laurel passed around a handful of clementine oranges to the girls, answering questions and pointing out God's beautiful world as they picnicked. Some of the questions the children asked both amused and amazed. The kids were smart and open and curious.

Today's weather wasn't as warm as she'd hoped and the sky was overcast, but the five members of her little Sunday school class didn't seem affected. Their high energy kept them warm, and she had been promising this outing for weeks.

Getting away from the newspaper office and Gran took careful organization. Today, she'd managed. At the rate the *Sundown Valley Times* was failing, one Sunday afternoon away would not change the downward trajectory.

She dug a thumbnail into her fresh-scented orange and had begun peeling away the thick covering when the nearby brush rustled.

The picnic group froze, eyes sliding first toward her and then around the clearing. She could read their minds. *Bears.* And in this mountain wilderness, black bears were a real possibility.

She put her arms out to each side as if she could shield the girls from an attack. She might lose, but she'd try.

Suddenly, the bushes parted, and a shaggy animal came into sight.

Chelsey screamed, "Bear!"

The other four girls jumped to their feet and screamed. One of them yelled, "Bigfoot!"

Not Bigfoot. A dog, followed by a tall, thin man in

camouflage pants, jacket and ball cap. He carried a fishing pole and a rifle.

Laurel squeaked. The girls screamed. The dog barked. The man rested the gear against his leg and tossed up both hands.

"I come in peace."

The dog, a real beauty that looked like a smaller version of a German shepherd, stood guard at the man's side. But his tail wagged faster than a windshield wiper on high.

Was he friendly? Was the man?

"Laurel," the bearded stranger said.

He knew her name?

"It's me," he said through a thick beard. "Yates. I didn't mean to startle you."

All the blood drained out of Laurel's head. She suffered a momentary dizzy spell.

"Yates?" Her voice came out shaky and bewildered. "You can't be here."

Yates Trudeau. The man she'd loved. The man who had left without a word.

Being a Bible-believing Christian, she couldn't hate him. But she was sorely tempted to kick him in the shins.

Except the dog might attack if she did.

And she had her Sunday school class with her. The little group now huddled close to her side like chicks under a hen. One glance down revealed five pairs of eyes locked on the tall man.

He tilted his head. "This is still my property, isn't it?"

She shook out the cobwebs. "I mean, you're in the army somewhere a world away."

With a hint at the old Yates's humor, the man slowly lowered his hands, patted his arms and his sides and pretended to look himself over. "No. I think this is me, and I'm definitely here."

He was Yates all right, but not Yates. The Yates she'd

known was vibrant with life, strong and healthy, a clean-cut cowboy exuding charm and energy. This man was thin and wan, with shaggy hair and a long beard that made him look like some old survivalist living off the land.

Was he?

No wonder the girls had thought he was Bigfoot. Sightings of the creature in the Kiamichi weren't that unusual. Sightings of long-lost loves absolutely were.

"What brings you home?" Was that the best she could do after eight years of wanting to scratch his eyes out?

Except she'd always loved his ocean-blue eyes—the way they softened right before he kissed her, the way they sparkled with laughter and intelligence.

"Mustered out." He nudged his chin toward the dog. "Justice and me both."

"You were a dog handler in the army?"

"No. Recon scout. But I knew him, and when he couldn't serve as MWD anymore, I put in the papers for him." He jerked a shoulder. "Didn't want a good soldier going civilian without a familiar face."

She had no idea what an MWD or a recon scout was, but a scout sounded like something on horseback, which would be right up Yates's alley. Did the military still ride horses?

"Is he friendly?"

"When I tell him to be."

She made a face. "That wasn't encouraging."

Yates squatted beside the dog and murmured something. Justice's tail increased in RPMs.

"Ladies." Yates looked up. "Justice won't hurt you. Would you like to shake his hand?"

Five cute heads bobbed up and down like yo-yos on a string.

Yates instructed the dog again. Justice approached the children and offered a paw, pink tongue lolling. Giggling, each girl took a turn.

Emboldened, Chelsey asked, "Can we pet him?"

"He'd like that." Yates reached into his pocket and pulled out a strange, bumpy-looking red rubber ball. "If you want to play with him, give this a toss."

The girls apparently had conquered their fear of the man, the dog and unseen bears.

While they romped with the delighted canine, Yates watched the dog. Laurel watched Yates.

Being a detail-oriented newspaper woman, she noticed everything about him, even the pine scent emanating from his clothes. She'd never seen anyone stand so still and silent. He was intense, to say the least. This certainly wasn't the Yates she had known.

There was pain in his eyes. The kind of pain she'd seen when his brother Trent had been tragically killed while feeding a pen of young bulls. But, either time hadn't healed that awful wound—and she didn't expect it would ever heal completely—or the military had added more pain for him to bear.

He appeared to be physically ill as well as in emotional pain. And he looked so terribly alone, like a lost soul.

What in the world had happened to him?

Every nurturing cell in her body wanted to rush into his life all over again and make everything better.

He was needy. She was a fixer.

And wouldn't the confident, always-in-command Yates of yesteryear mock such an idea?

She was out of her mind to even consider getting involved with a Trudeau again.

"You don't look well." Why had she said that? Why couldn't she keep her thoughts to herself?

Yates's shaggy head snapped back to face her.

"Had a couple of surgeries."

"What happened?"

He waved a hand as if shooing away the question. "No big deal. I'm okay now."

In other words, don't pry, which only made a newspaper woman more curious. Add to that the fact that he didn't *look* okay and her nose for news fairly twitched.

"I guess Wade and Bowie are thrilled to have you home." She was fishing for information the way she'd once done with big-city politicians. Ask the right, seemingly harmless questions, and sometimes the important stuff seeped out. But that was before Dad had died and she inherited a small-town newspaper.

"Haven't seen them yet," he said.

"You haven't been to the ranch? Did you just arrive in town and suddenly decide to go for a hike before seeing your family? Who does that?" The words tumbled out, as they often did when she was interviewing. Which she wasn't. "Sorry. Nosey reporter's habit."

"No problem." His look was as solemn as a funeral. He did not, she noticed with suspicion, respond to either of her queries.

Had he really come to the woods before going to the ranch house? She had a feeling she was right and that he had. She wondered why—another habit of journalists. She needed to know everything, especially motives.

Yates's gaze seemed glued to her face, and she fought off a blush that would let him know he still affected her on some unwanted, visceral level. People say you always remember your first love. Yates had been her first and only.

She'd spent the better part of a year waiting to hear from him and another year getting over him.

Now here he was in the flesh, stirring up old memories. At least for her.

The annoying blush deepened. Laurel turned her attention toward the children and the dog. With a smiling

Justice in the center, they formed a circle of petting hands and eager chatter.

"Those aren't all your kids, are they?"

A small pain pinched inside her chest. "Sunday school class." To turn the focus away from her, she asked, "Was he really a military dog? Like a bomb or drug sniffer?"

"Explosives."

"Did something happen to him? Why'd he retire?"

Yates's face, already closed, tightened. "Stuff happens. Soldiers retire. Look, I should go. Enjoy your picnic."

With a snappy military about-face, he started to walk away.

"Yates, wait."

He paused, gazing back over his shoulder.

"After you get settled, come by the *Times*' office. I'd love to interview you and the dog for the paper." She put her fingers up in air quotes. "'Hometown Hero Returns' would make a great feature."

"No interview. We're civilians now. Nothing heroic about that." Turning away, he gave a soft whistle. "Justice, come."

Before she could say more, Yates and his dog disappeared into the foliage.

Chapter Two

"You'd better wait in the truck for now."

Yates signaled the dog to stay as he exited the vehicle. Not knowing what he was about to step into made him cautious.

Striding toward his childhood home, his heart clattered in his chest like a schoolboy picking up his first date. Sundown Ranch had changed some. He'd expected that. Wade was a sharp businessman, and he and Bowie were both real good at cowboying.

The air smelled the same, like hay and the pine trees that grew along the driveway. Someone had fixed up the old bunkhouse.

Yellow early-spring flowers once again sprouted from tidy beds lining the sides of the main ranch-style house the way they had when Mom was alive. Wade's wife, he supposed. Wade wasn't into flowers much. If it didn't feed cows and horses, he didn't grow it.

They'd added a couple more barns and new fences, and painted the horse barn a deep red. Slick, fat, black cattle grazed in the rapidly greening pastures. Calves cavorted, tails whipping over their shiny backs.

Yates wondered about his horses. Were they long gone, sold when he hadn't returned home?

Not that he could ride. Maybe he never would again.

He wasn't sure he could bear to live here on the ranch without riding horses.

Yates stepped up on the long concrete porch, letting his hand sweep over the railing. He recalled helping his dad stain the wooden slats—a tedious task—though now the entire railing was painted white. Someone had painted the door a bright blue too.

The changes bothered him, made him feel more of a stranger than he was.

Yates reached for the doorbell, then let his hand drop, uncertain of protocol. Thanks to the army, he preferred protocol, clear-cut rules, knowing what to do when.

Should he go on inside the way he'd done in the past, without knocking? This house was one-third his. He'd grown up here, had lived here until he'd joined the army.

Maybe he should ring the bell. He'd been gone a long time. Wade's wife didn't know him from Adam.

He removed his cap and ran a hand through his shaggy hair, searching for his bearings. Laurel hadn't recognized him at first. She'd screamed. Well, not screamed exactly, but she'd made a sound that let him know his appearance shocked her. Maybe he should have shaved, gotten a haircut.

He started to turn away.

A lock clicked and the door swung open. Too late to leave now.

"May I help you?" Before he could answer, the redhead sucked in a little gasp and put a hand to her mouth. "Yates? Are you Yates?"

"You must be Kyra. I hear my brother is looking for me."

She reached out and plucked his sleeve. "Come in. I'll get Wade. And text Bowie. Oh, they'll be so happy."

She disappeared down the hall, heading, he figured, to the ranch's home office, where his brother Wade would be plying his business acumen.

Yates stood in the flower-scented entryway, feeling as out of place as if he'd never been here before. Awkward.

Wishing he'd gone back to the camper in Centerville and put this meeting off another day or two.

But he was no coward. Now that the newspaper woman, Laurel, knew he was back, he was taking no chances she'd spill the beans first. He owed his family that much.

He heard chattering voices just before a small child toddled into sight, followed by two more. He experienced a rush of shame, having forgotten about Wade's triplets. Yates had never met them. Or the first wife who'd abandoned them.

The three tiny kids, all resembling Wade, stopped when they spotted Yates. The little girl in pink overalls said, "Hi."

"Hi."

The word must have contained some kind of activation message, because all three proceeded in his direction. What was he supposed to do? Hunker down? Dodge and run?

Before he could figure out his next move, his brother appeared from a doorway off to the left of the entry hall.

The bottom fell out of his belly. A yearning as big as the outdoors stretched inside him.

Wade. His brother. His best friend. Until he wasn't.

"It's really you." Wade stormed at him, a man on a mission. Yates braced both knees for the incoming missile. Punch or hug, he'd take either without complaint.

In seconds, Wade's strong rancher's arms enveloped him, patting him on the back hard enough to collapse a lung.

Regret washed through Yates. He stepped back from the warm welcome. He didn't deserve it. "Good to see you."

"Really good." Wade's eyes, the same shape and clear-blue color as his, shone with pleasure. "Man, I've missed you. You're finally home."

"I am." No choice in the matter. He was no longer fit for service. Or much of anything else.

"Great. We could use your help around here."

The remark worried Yates. How would he keep his problem to himself without looking like a slacker? A man had his pride, and he hadn't come home to cry on his family's shoulders or ask them to take care of him if he couldn't take care of himself.

Why *had* he come home?

Familiarity, maybe? Though too much was *not* familiar. Like Wade's sweet-faced, red-haired wife.

Kyra and the triplets hovered nearby. She beamed as if she was as happy about his return as Wade. And she didn't even know him. But she loved his brother, and his brother wanted him to come home. Yates had saved the texts and emails to remind him of as much.

"This redhead is Kyra, my beautiful, incredible bride," Wade said with pride and affection. "And these are the Trudeau nuggets." He placed a hand on each head as he named them. "Abby the talker, Ben the bold, and Caden the cuddler."

What did a man say to kids whose language was mostly gibberish?

He gave a short nod toward Kyra. "Nice to meet you, ma'am."

She smiled. "Kyra. Welcome home, Yates."

At that moment, his cousin Bowie burst through the back door and barreled through the kitchen toward him.

Yates's heart leaped to see him again. Bowie—the quiet, steady one of the bunch—repeated Wade's man hug and back slaps. In the process, the cowboy knocked his gray Stetson from his head. Laughing, he bent down to retrieve it, then turned it upside down on top of the narrow credenza in the entry.

"You guys go in the living room and catch up," Kyra said. "The triplets and I will bring refreshments."

Yates's belly reminded him that he'd yet to eat today. Too many interruptions. "Thanks. Refreshments sound good."

A T-bone steak sounded better. The thought surprised him, given that he'd had very little appetite since the blast that put him in the hospital. No one was enticed to fill up on hospital food.

Kyra and the kids disappeared. Yates followed his brothers into the big living space. Toys were scattered on the blue-patterned area rug. A light gray sectional replaced the old black couch where he had liked to nap. Pictures of babies and a wedding decorated the fireplace mantel.

Things had changed. So had he.

Had he changed too much to make a life here again?

With the enemy lurking in his spine, did he dare try?

Where else would he go? What could he do besides wait for the grim future to catch him?

He had no answers. At least here he had a vested interest. He owned one-third of a large, successful cattle ranch.

An old adage scrolled through his head.

Home is the place where, when you've got no place else to go, they have to take you in.

He'd never doubted that for a minute, although the issue of Trent's death was a silent wedge between him and his brother. He needed to confess everything, but he wouldn't. Couldn't. Dragging Laurel's name into his mess was plain wrong. Wade already had hard feelings toward the Keno clan. They all did. None of that trouble was Laurel's fault.

The three men settled in various chairs. Yates stretched his long legs out in front of him, though he was anything but relaxed.

An uncomfortable silence followed. What was he supposed to say or do? What did they expect from him? What did he expect from *them*?

"So," Wade declared, leaning forward with his forearms on his knees. "What gives? Why are you hiding in the woods like some weirdo?"

Weirdo?

Yates bristled.

"I wasn't hiding," he said with more than a touch of irritation.

"Sure looked like it to us. You didn't answer phone calls. Rarely answered texts or emails. Most of the time, we had no idea if you were dead or alive."

Yates flinched at the word *dead*. He'd never wanted them to worry about him; but with his specialty, he'd always been in danger. "Didn't want to worry you."

"Well, you failed at that, didn't you?"

"Hey. Hey." Bowie rose and placed a hand on Wade's shoulder. In his calm, quiet manner, he said, "Ease off, Wade. Give him some space. He's home. Isn't that what we wanted? What we prayed for?"

Wade raked a hand through his hair, exactly as he'd done for as long as Yates could remember. That, at least, hadn't changed. Neither had Wade's propensity for losing his cool.

"You're right. But I just…"

Bowie patted his shoulder. "Kill the fatted calf. This is a celebration."

Yates recognized the reference. They considered him a prodigal. He guessed he was, at least to them. To Uncle Sam, he'd been important. Now he didn't know what he was.

He should have gone somewhere else when he'd left the army. But where? This was home.

"The ranch looks in good shape."

"What did you expect? That we'd let it fall apart because you weren't here?"

Wade still had a burr under his saddle.

Yates tensed but kept his voice steady. As the oldest, the expectation had been that he would run the ranch; but he had walked away, leaving Wade in command. "I knew it was in good hands. You were better at the business side of ranching than I could ever be."

Wade's mouth opened and then closed, then opened again. "No one sits a horse like you."

The reminder, meant as a compliment, sliced through Yates like a meat cleaver.

"Been a long time. Things around here have changed."

"Be glad to give you a tour," Bowie said. "I think you'll be pleased."

"We didn't squander your inheritance." Wade laughed. "Or ours."

"I don't expect anything. You've done all the work."

"Too bad." Bowie snitched a potato chip as Kyra entered the room with a tray of sandwiches and chips. His wide, beautifully tooled watchband served as a reminder of his leather artistry. "Wade kept a separate ledger and bank account for your share."

Which made Yates feel all the guiltier. "Thanks. You didn't have to."

"Dad would have," Wade said. "Now that you're back, I expect you to pull your weight around here. Make up for lost time."

Yates liked the sound of that. He just wasn't sure he could.

"He hasn't said yet if he's staying." Bowie narrowed dark eyes in his direction. "Are you?"

"Or is this just a little visit before you run off again and we don't see you for eight long years?" According to Wade's curt tone, he was still mad. He had a right to be.

Fact of the matter, he had a right to despise Yates as much as he despised the neighboring Kenos.

Which brought Laurel to mind. Her grandmother had been born a Keno. She was off-limits to anyone named Trudeau. He hadn't let that stop him then—had even considered it a fun challenge—and look how that had turned out.

"I'm home to stay, if you'll have me. No plans yet. Still getting my strength back after surgery."

Wade straightened. "Surgery? Is that why you look like a cadaver?"

"Wade, stop." Kyra's voice held an edge. She might be sweet and loving, but there was steel in the woman. Yates liked her.

"What happened, Yates?" She handed him a sandwich and a napkin when he didn't take one on his own. "Were you injured in combat?"

"Something like that. I'd prefer not to talk about it, if you don't mind."

"Of course. You need time to rest and adjust. The details can wait." A kind smile brightened her pretty face. "We're happy you're home. I'll make up the guest room for you."

With a slight frown, Yates tilted his head. "What about my old bedroom?"

"Sorry." Kyra's expression turned apologetic. "It's a nursery now."

Right. More change.

"Whatever's convenient, then. Or I can go back to Centerville."

When the others lifted their eyebrows in question, he added, "I have a fifth-wheel RV parked outside of Centerville."

"We want you here, Yates," Bowie said softly. "Home."

Home that wasn't home.

Yates pushed up from the chair, needing air, needing to think—to get away from the tsunami of changes and memories. "Think I'll get my dog and take a walk, reacquaint myself with the ranch."

"Want company?" Bowie asked.

He tried to smile at his kindhearted cousin but figured his look was more of a grimace. Which was how he felt about company right now. "Not this time."

Adjusting to civilian life was going to be harder than he'd expected. And he hadn't expected it to be easy.

* * *

A woman shouldn't wish for a crime to be committed, but on this chilly spring morning, the idea crossed Laurel's mind more than once.

That's how badly she needed a strong paper-selling news story.

"Are we going under?" The worried question came from Tansy Winchell, who was Laurel's best friend as well as the *Times'* assistant editor and jack-of-all-trades.

Laurel clenched her jaw with determination, but her belly jittered, every bit as anxious as her friend. "Over my dead body."

As owner and publisher of Sundown Valley's only daily paper, Laurel had watched the newspaper business dwindle with the addition of every new app and social media outlet. Newspapers were becoming a thing of the past. Dinosaurs. Obsolete.

An older woman stuck her curly gray-haired head around the door dividing the long layout room from Laurel's inner office. Myra Zachary had worked at the paper longer than anyone. She'd been a stringer for Laurel's father, George Maxwell, as a teenager during the newspaper's heyday, when every person in Sundown Valley and all the surrounding areas subscribed.

In a voice that sounded as if her vocal cords had gone through a meat grinder, Myra barked, "Your daddy would be heartbroken if we lost the *Times.*"

Sometimes Laurel was glad Dad hadn't lived to see this steady decline. But not often. Most of the time, she missed him with an ache big enough to fill Blue Lake. And that was big.

George Maxwell had been a hard-driving journalist and a no-nonsense father whose high expectations for his only child still echoed in her head. She couldn't let him down.

The only time she'd ever gone against his will was with

Yates Trudeau. Though Dad had never known about the secret romance, she'd paid dearly for her disobedience.

"Subscriptions have fallen again this month," Laurel said, "but that doesn't mean we're throwing in the towel."

"An all-time low, Laurel," Myra said. "We're bleeding subscribers. And money."

"We have to come up with some way to lure people back." Forehead tight with worry, Laurel rose from her desk and the troubling statistics to pace around the tiny office.

The scent of newsprint was in her nose and in her blood. She couldn't imagine her life without it.

Tansy—whose purple-and-pink-striped hair, clunky combat boots and funny T-shirts usually cheered a more conventional Laurel—pushed over-size black-framed glasses higher on her nose. "What if we can't?"

Laurel arched an eyebrow. "Pessimism, Tansy? From you? I don't need that right now. Isn't there a story somewhere in this town that you can write?"

Tansy slapped a folder down on her desk. "You've been cranky all morning. What's the deal?"

Yates Trudeau was Laurel's first thought. Seeing him had rattled every bone in her body. She'd lain awake half the night thinking about him, about them, about the past and how he'd hurt her. Then this morning's negative numbers had pushed her over the edge.

"I'm not cranky."

Tansy made one of her faces that said exactly what she thought of Laurel's statement. "I'm going to the Bea Sweet Bakery to get you some doughnuts. You need some serious sweetening."

As a parting shot intended to break the mood, Tansy stuck out her tongue and disappeared.

In spite of her worry, Laurel snickered. Having a life-long best friend as an employee was both a challenge and a blessing. Tansy literally knew her better than anyone on earth.

And she was right. Ms. Bea's chocolate doughnuts sounded really good right now. Laurel went to the coffeepot and filled her cup before adding a sprinkle of sweetener. Then she returned to her desk to begin editing tomorrow's edition.

Her cell phone rang. She ignored it. She was busy and assumed it was Tansy asking if she wanted a loaf of some outrageously delicious and fattening specialty bread that Sage Walker had baked. That woman's baking skills could add pounds to a marble statue.

A too-thin Yates Trudeau jumped into her head. Again. The gaunt and pale former soldier troubled her. Not that she had any business being concerned about him. Yet what had happened to him, and why didn't he want to talk about it? And why on earth did she even care after eight years of silence?

Ugh. Curiosity. Some days it drove her nuts.

No wonder she was cranky.

The glass door to the entrance breezed open. She knew this because cool air suddenly swished and swirled around her ankles.

Tansy bopped into her office, toting the familiar white bakery box. Whipping open the lid, she waved the contents under Laurel's nose.

"Smell that chocolate, boss lady," Tansy said, "and admit that I am the most awesome best friend you've ever had."

"The only one I've ever had. Right now, you're my favorite." Snagging a chocolate long John, Laurel savored a sweet, chocolaty bite, then dunked the jagged edge into her coffee.

"Ew." Tansy shuddered. "I don't know how you do that. Wet doughnut. So disgusting."

"Delicious." Laurel grinned and bit into the now-coffee-flavored treat. "How were things at the bakery?"

"Hopping. The line was out the door."

"No surprise there. The Bea Sweet has always been the morning gathering place, though I have noticed an increase in traffic since Sage Walker started working with Ms. Bea."

"That's because two people can bake more yummy stuff. The bakery was getting to be too much for Ms. Bea, especially after her arthritis got so bad and she fell."

"True. I'm glad Sage moved back to town." Having a bakery right next door to the newspaper office saved time. And, Laurel thought wryly, overindulged her sweet tooth.

Blessings and challenges. Didn't Jesus say we'd have both in this world?

"Bowie Trudeau is glad Sage is back too." Tansy picked colored sprinkles from a glazed doughnut. "Did you know they got engaged?"

Laurel blinked a couple of times. Was there some kind of conspiracy afoot today to make her think about the Trudeau men?

"I'd heard that. I wonder if they'll want to put an engagement announcement in the paper."

She'd run an article on Wade and Kyra's wedding, even though she'd most definitely not been invited to the ceremony. Kyra, a friendly woman, had stopped in with the information. Wade had not accompanied her. No surprise there.

That ridiculous Keno-versus-Trudeau feud. Neither she nor Yates had known what caused the rift, and yet it continued. Kenos blamed Trudeaus. Trudeaus blamed Kenos. And on it went, generation after generation.

"I'll ask Sage about an announcement when I go back for the amazingly fragrant bread she had in the oven."

"A moment on the lips. Forever on the hips."

Tansy wiggled her pale eyebrows. "I'll grab a loaf for you too."

When Laurel didn't protest, Tansy chortled knowingly, placed two more doughnuts on a napkin and shoved them toward her before taking the box and making the rounds in the newsroom. No matter the circumstances, Tansy Winchell found a way to bring cheer.

Laurel watched her friend through the plate glass. Tansy had every reason to be a grouchy, depressing whiner. Her life had not been an easy one. But she exuded Jesus-like qualities. *Lemons to lemonade* was Tansy's mantra.

An idea formed as Laurel's mind strayed again to yesterday's unexpected meeting with Yates. He was a lemon in her life. He was also an opportunity for lemonade.

"Tansy!"

Tansy appeared in the doorway, a doughnut in each hand. "What?"

"Close my door. I have an idea to run past you."

Tansy, who never seemed to gain an ounce, shoved in another bite and shut the door. "What's up?"

Laurel took a deep breath. "I saw Yates Trudeau yesterday."

Tansy was the only other person who knew the history behind that statement.

The best friend choked on her doughnut, coughing until her eyes watered. Lauren started to rise, but Tansy waved her off.

When she'd regained her composure, she grabbed a chair, dragged it close to Laurel's and lowered her voice in a conspiratorial tone. "Spill it. Tell all. Did you leave him alive? With all limbs intact?"

"I'm over him, Tansy. That isn't why I'm telling you."

"Right." Tansy clearly did not believe her.

Ignoring the little worry that maybe her friend was correct, Laurel revealed the impromptu meeting in the woods.

"How does he look? Is he still dreamy handsome, with those piercing blue eyes and all those lean cowboy muscles?"

"He looks awful."

Tansy clapped her hands. "Oh goody."

"I'm serious, Tansy. He's had some kind of injury, and he's so thin and gaunt he'd disappear if he turned sideways. It's sad."

"Sorry." Tansy looked repentant. "You know I would never disparage a wounded warrior if he hadn't hurt you so badly."

"Long time ago." Laurel flicked a hand out to one side as if flicking away a piece of lint. "The thing is, his return and his injury are news. The Trudeau name carries clout in this county, and a wounded-soldier story is a powerful, emotional hook. An article about Yates will sell papers."

As if flying a banner in the sky, she moved a hand from one side to the other. "'Hometown Hero Returns.' Or something to that effect. Plus, he has a military dog. Dogs sell. What do you think?"

"You are brilliant. Call him and ask for an interview."

"I asked. He said no."

Tansy waved her remaining doughnut. "I doubt if he meant it. People love to see their names in the paper. He was being modest."

"Maybe." Though she'd never known Yates to be especially modest about his accomplishments. And he was good at lots of things. Training horses. Kissing.

A flush heated her cheeks. Why had she thought about *that*?

"We're desperate for a strong lead, Laurel. A hero's return is big news in Sundown Valley, especially if his last name is Trudeau. Townspeople know their tragic background. They'd be interested."

"Gran would have a fit if she knew I'd been within a mile of a Trudeau." So would her dad.

"That silly feud again? Do you think your grandma knows the cause? You should ask."

"If she knows, she's not telling, but she and Dad drilled it into my head from toddler stage that Trudeaus were bad, Kenos were good. Steer clear."

"So you went and fell in love with a Trudeau. You rebel."

"Don't remind me." Laurel huffed out a frustrated sigh, torn between needing a story and opening up a can of worms.

An office phone rang somewhere in the building. Myra's rusty-throated voice reached her ears. "Pick up, Laurel. It's your grandmother."

Tansy rose, pointing the half-eaten doughnut at Laurel. "I heard your dad say a hundred times, follow the story. Yates won't mind. He'll be flattered."

With that encouraging reminder, Tansy and her heavy boots clomped out of the office.

Mind swirling with uncertainty, Laurel punched the blinking light on the old-fashioned desk phone. The black touch-tone was the same one her dad had used, and she was downright sentimental about it. "Gran, are you okay?"

"Why didn't you answer your cell phone?"

"Was that you? I'm sorry. I was busy."

Gran made an irritated sound, though with her breathing issues, she always sounded annoyed and breathless. "I can't find my pills. What did you do with them?"

"In your pill planner, like every day."

"Well, I can't find them." Gran's breath grew shorter. "You'll have to come home. My arm hurts. I need my pills."

A frisson of alarm prickled the hair on Laurel's scalp. Arm pain was not good for someone with heart problems.

"Listen to me, Gran. Sit down and stay there. Make sure your oxygen tube isn't kinked, and then think about something good until I arrive. Okay?"

"Okay. Now, don't drive…fast… I'm just…out of breath."

Which was exactly the problem.

"Love you, Gran." Laurel hung up, grabbed her keys from the top desk drawer and hollered her destination to whoever was listening as she rushed out the door.

Once she reached the craftsman bungalow in the quiet residential cul-de-sac where she'd grown up, Laurel found Gran's pill planner under the edge of the kitchen counter. She must have knocked it off and forgotten. Usually her mind was sharp as a new pencil, but the octogenarian had forgetful moments.

Gran, toting her portable oxygen, wandered into the kitchen.

As she filled a glass with water, Laurel studied the woman who'd helped Dad raise her. Gran's color was ashen in spite of her heavy red lipstick. Laurel wanted to scold the older woman for not remaining in her chair, but dire warnings proved useless.

"Don't frown," Gran said. "You'll get wrinkles."

"You're out of your chair."

Gran pumped her elbow. Her fleshy triceps jiggled. "My arm is better now. No pain."

Laurel sighed and handed over the pills and water.

Gran obediently downed the medication and then took a minute to catch her breath. Her gaze, as sharp as her personality, roved over Laurel.

Laurel braced herself. Here it came: the weekly lecture. Either about valuing and furthering the legacy her father had left her or improving her appearance.

"Go press that skirt, girl, and put on some lipstick. You'll never catch a man looking like an unmade bed."

Laurel stared down at her rumpled skirt. She absolutely did not have time for this.

"I'm not trying to attract a man, Gran."

"Obviously. You haven't had a date since David Rymer took you to the Valentine Ball."

Three years ago? Had it really been that long?

"Single guys my age are in short supply."

Her annoying mind went straight to Yates Trudeau. Seeing him again, especially in his weakened condition, affected her more than she wanted to admit.

She would not think about that or him until she got back to the office. And then only because he would make a good news story.

Gran would have a fit if she knew Laurel had shared a civil conversation with a Trudeau.

Gran was right about one thing, though. Laurel was getting old, over the hill. Most of her friends had been married for a long time and had children. She'd wanted that, too, but it hadn't happened. She'd once dreamed of a life with Yates. After he left, something in her had stopped believing in happy-ever-after, except in her beloved romance novels.

Maybe God wanted her to remain single, like the apostle Paul. Except she was no evangelist—just a small-town newspaper editor rooming with an obstinate, grudge-holding grandma and trying to live for the Lord the best she could.

She put the used drinking glass into the dishwasher, eager to get back to work.

Gran's lecture wasn't finished. When she got on a topic, she was like a biting turtle that wouldn't turn loose until lightning struck.

"So rob the cradle. What is it they call an older woman with a younger man these days? A cougar?"

Laurel snorted. "I'm no cougar, Gran."

"You could be if you'd press that skirt and wear some lipstick. And stop frowning. You'll get squinch-eyed."

Laurel looked toward the ceiling and shook her head. She had no idea what squinch-eyed was, but, like running with scissors, it was a dire warning Gran had leveled in her direction since she'd found Laurel reading under the covers with a pin light at age eight.

Arguing was senseless.

Leaning in to kiss Gran's cheek, she said, "Be sure to eat your lunch. Thirty seconds in the microwave. Call if you need me."

The other woman sniffed. "You won't answer."

"Just call, Gran. I love you. I have to get back to work and find a strong story."

"Sales down again this month?"

"Yes."

"We need more violence in this town."

Laurel laughed, then chided, "Gran," even though she'd thought the same thing.

Gran grinned an ornery grin before growing serious. "Your daddy worked his tail off to build that newspaper. Don't let him down."

"I can't make up stories, Gran."

"Some do—especially these days."

"Not us. Daddy was a true journalist and trained me to be the same."

"Then go find a good, strong story for the lead and write it."

Laurel didn't have to find a story. She had one.

And Gran had just given her the push she needed to make it happen.

Chapter Three

Horsehide had to be his favorite scent of all time.

Yates leaned both forearms on top of the railing outside the horse barn and watched three quarter horse mares nibble at patches of barely sprouted green grass. Everything in him wanted to throw a saddle over one of them and ride. Forget the fear and the dire warnings, and ride the wind.

Near his left thigh, Justice sat watching the horses with the same comfortable interest as his owner. Trained to ignore distractions, the dog had encountered everything from goats to snakes to llamas during his career without a mistake. Horses didn't faze him.

Behind him, Yates heard the crunch of boots on the gravel driveway.

Justice rose to his feet. Yates dropped a reassuring hand to the pointed ears. They were home now. No need to get tense about footsteps.

Bowie's muscled forearms joined Yates's scrawny ones on the railing. The contrast was not lost on Yates. He'd always been the strongest and fittest, and he was eager to rebuild what his injury had stolen.

Except some things would never heal.

"Each year we saved back the youngest three mares in case you wanted to start up again someday. We kept hoping." Bowie's soft voice held a yearning that said Yates had been missed more than he'd known. Definitely more than he deserved.

"Thank you. They're beauties." Yates cleared his throat, grateful. During the last twenty-four hours, emotion had snuck up on him, caught him off guard. He was still trying to sort it all out. "What about Excalibur?"

The stallion colt, out of the best bloodlines in the country, had been the future of his dream horse farm. But that was before Trent died.

"Couldn't let him go, knowing how much he meant to you. He's matured into a beautiful animal."

Nine years old now—prime adulthood for a stud horse. "How do his colts look?"

"Top notch. They're sold before they hit the ground." Bowie dropped his boot from the bottom rail and shifted in Yates's direction. "Feel up to riding yet? You could get a close-up look at the ranch and the livestock."

"Not today." Maybe not ever. Not that he would admit as much to Bowie or Wade. The last thing he wanted was their sad-eyed pity. "I'm still not a hundred percent."

The comment was laughable considering the way he looked, but Bowie's expression remained serious.

"Understandable. You need some meat on those bones." Bowie removed his hat and studied the inside. "You never said what kind of injury you had."

That's because he was afraid of revealing too much. If he disclosed the number and locations of the surgeries, more questions would follow, and soon, they'd know too much. His family had lost enough in their lives. He'd spare them one more worry.

Before he could formulate a sidestepping reply, a truck door slammed, and both men pivoted toward the sound.

Wade stalked toward them across the graveled space.

Yates sighed. What now? His brother had had a bee in his bonnet since Yates's arrival. Prickly as a porcupine.

"What's up?" Bowie asked as they walked out to meet

Wade. Pudge, the ranch's blue heeler cow dog, remained in the pickup.

"The usual. Number-four gate open, the lock cut. Cows on the road."

Yates's belly tightened. "Kenos?"

After the encounter with Laurel on Sunday afternoon, he'd tried to put her and her troublesome family out of his mind. They didn't seem inclined to stay away.

"Always."

Yates sighed. Many things had changed, but not this— the one thing that needed to change the most. "So the feud goes on."

"Their doing. We don't cut fences or locks, or dam up creeks. They get their laughs with that kind of mischief."

True, and he'd gotten Trudeau revenge at Laurel's expense, actions that haunted him still. What had begun on a lark had turned to something else entirely, and he'd been too messed up to know what to do about it. About her.

"Any animals escape?" Bowie asked.

"A few I rounded up. Riley took the ATV to double-check for strays."

"Riley?" Yates asked.

"Hired hand. Good friend now. You'll like him. We needed help after you left, and Riley wanted to cowboy."

Wade may not have intended to jab at his conscience, but Yates felt it anyway.

When Yates didn't reply, Wade kept talking. "I figure we should take a look at the other gates and fences to be on the safe side. Want to ride fence today?"

That question again. It drove him nuts. Of course he wanted to ride. Wade and Bowie knew how much he loved being in the saddle. That's why they asked. But he couldn't, not unless he wanted to be paralyzed for the rest of his life.

He shook his head. "It may be a while before I'm up to it."

Wade narrowed his eyes, gazing at him for a long, un-comfortable minute as if he suspected there was more to Yates's refusal that he wasn't saying. His brother was right, of course.

"Kyra said you skipped breakfast."

"Wanted to see the horses first."

Wade huffed. "Yeah. You wanted to see *them*, but when your only living brother got married, you were nowhere around."

The burr in Wade's saddle was aimed at him again. Maybe the dig about hiring Riley in his place had been intentional after all.

"I was there."

Wade scoffed. "Sure you were."

Bowie put a warning hand on Wade's arm. "If he says he was—"

"I was." Yates clenched and unclenched his fists. The same hot blood that ran through Wade ran through Yates. He just controlled it better.

"The wedding took place last fall, near the park pavil-ion overlooking the canyon. Bowie and another guy were groomsmen. Gray vests, blue jeans, mint-green ties. An ugly lot, but you cleaned up good."

He tossed in the last because he knew Bowie and Wade would consider the insult a compliment. It had been.

Wade blinked. "But where? I didn't see you."

Yates looked down at his camo pants and jacket. He felt more natural in them than the stiff jeans he'd once con-sidered standard attire. He knew how to remain unseen.

"Stayed out of sight, along the tree line. I wasn't ex-actly dressed for a fancy wedding. The barbecue smell was tempting, though."

"That was you!" Bowie said, suddenly animated. "Riley and I spotted a man standing on the east side of the park.

At first, we suspected a Keno, but the description didn't fit any we knew. Way too skinny."

Yates's shoulder hitched. "I was back in the States. Couldn't miss my brother's wedding when I was this close."

He had missed a lot of other things too. For once, Wade kept his mouth shut and didn't remind him.

In a calmer tone, Wade said, "I'm glad you were there. More than that, I'm glad you're home. I'm just sorry—" His voice lowered, remorseful. "I know you blame me for Trent's accident—"

"No!" Yates whirled on him. "We aren't going to talk about that."

Wade instantly bristled again, stepping closer.

"Why not?" he yelled. "It's the elephant in the room."

Bowie put a hand on each man's chest as if holding them apart. Maybe he was, though Yates would never raise a hand to his brother.

Yates took a deep breath and said the only thing he dared. "I don't blame you."

Wade scoffed, eyes still blazing blue fire. "Yeah, well, eight years of silence says you're lying."

"Easy, boys." Bowie's dark gaze locked on Wade. In his steady, sensible and ever-soft voice, he said, "We prayed about this, Wade. Agreed to give Yates all the grace he needed. He's home. That's all that matters."

They'd talked about him behind his back?

"Yeah. Yeah. I know." Wade yanked off his hat and raked a hand through his brown hair. "It's just that having him home brings it all back."

Wade didn't know the half of it, and Yates couldn't tell him.

The dog had moved to Yates's side, the fur standing up on his neck. Everything ran down chain, as the military handlers liked to say. Justice understood strong emotion, and if a threat was perceived, he'd defend Yates to the death.

Yates dropped a reassuring hand to the dog's head. "Want me to leave?"

"No!" A frown the size of Sundown Canyon creased Wade's forehead. "I never wanted you to leave in the first place."

"All right, now, you two." Bowie, ever the peacemaker, raised both palms. "I invited Sage and the kids for dinner tonight. You have to stop snapping at each other. Don't embarrass me in front of her."

"Sage?" Yates pivoted toward his cousin. "Sage Walker?"

"Yep." A soft, almost sappy smile bloomed on Bowie's darkly handsome face. "She's my fiancée now."

A grin broke through Yates's tension. "About time."

He'd dated Sage Walker exactly twice before he realized his favorite cousin was wildly, secretly in love with her. "Is she still knock-your-hat-in-the-dirt beautiful?"

"Even more so, but don't go getting any funny ideas." Bowie grinned when he said it, letting Yates know he was confident in his woman. "She's mine."

"Always was." Yates gave him a friendly rap on the shoulder. "You were both just too young and naive to know it. What's this about kids?"

"Sage's niece and nephew. She has guardianship."

"You're gonna be a daddy?"

"Looks that way, at least for a while—but I wouldn't mind forever. They're great kids."

With a rueful head shake, Yates surprised himself by joking, "All my rowdy friends have settled down."

Bowie chuckled. "You're next."

Yates's slightly improved mood plummeted again, but he kept his tone light and easy. "Not happening."

No woman wanted a man with a ticking time bomb in

his body. Even if she did, Yates would never saddle some-one he loved with an invalid.

"That's what *we* said, and now look at us." Wade clapped him on the back. "We better get to work. Do you feel up to driving a truck around the section lines?"

"Sure. Justice and I can handle that."

Justice, having heard his name, pressed closer to Yates's leg, ready to report for duty.

"Bowie and I will ride the inside pastures." Wade plopped his hat back on his head and adjusted it. "Check-ing everything may take most of the day. Let's grab some water and grub before we head out. You need to eat."

Three abreast, the way they'd done as teenagers, the trio crossed the barnyard and the gravel driveway and then went inside the house, where they began piling meat and cheese onto slices of wheat bread. The smell of spicy mustard mingled with pungent dill pickles, the scents of their childhood lunch pails. Trudeau eating habits, at least, had remained the same.

Justice flopped down on the cool tile with a bored sigh. The dog wanted to work. Like Yates, he missed doing his job. Yates broke feeding protocol and tossed him a chunk of ham.

Kyra came into the kitchen, a sniffling child on one hip. He was one of the look-alike boys, but Yates hadn't yet learned which was which.

"Ben's getting too big for you to carry, Kyra," Wade said. "You'll hurt your back again."

Again? Did Kyra have back issues too?

"My back is fine, honey. Benjamin bumped his head and got a boo-boo. He needed some extra love and a sippy of juice."

Wade reached for the boy, who pressed his face into his daddy's neck. With a tenderness Wade hadn't shown in the past, he patted the baby's back and murmured sweet encouragements.

"You're okay, buddy. Daddy's got you."

Emotion bubbled up in Yates. It was starting to annoy him, this sudden tendency to feel too much at once.

Kyra handed the toddler a small plastic cup with a spout. A sippy, Yates assumed. Once Benjamin was pacified, she opened the large walk-in pantry and brought out a bag of chips, which she placed on the granite counter beside the growing stack of sandwiches.

Yates helped himself to a slice of cheese. His appetite was still iffy, but he'd force himself to eat.

"Have you seen today's paper?" Kyra asked.

Wade kissed the top of Ben's head and slid him to the floor. The now-comforted child wandered off, toting his orange sippy cup.

"No, why?" Wade began sliding sandwiches into zippered bags.

The redhead held up an index finger. "Be right back."

The men exchanged glances. Wade shrugged.

Kyra returned, placing a folded newspaper on the countertop.

She tapped a pink-nailed finger on the black and white print. "Look who made the front page of the *Sundown Valley Times*."

"Who?"

Three male heads leaned in.

Yates blinked a few times before his brain comprehended what his eyes were seeing.

It was a photo of him. A muscular, fit image of himself in full combat gear.

He yanked the paper from the counter and shook it fully open. "Wounded Warrior Returns Home." The byline was Laurel Maxwell.

Fury rose in him like a tidal wave. She'd written an article anyway. Without his permission.

"Guess what?"

"What?" Laurel responded to Tansy's routine guessing game without looking up from her desk.

"I just got off the phone with Franklin IGA. They're asking for more newspapers."

The small-town grocery store displayed the papers at the checkout counter as a courtesy to customers and the *Times*. They rarely sold out anymore.

"Already?" Laurel pushed her computer screen to one side to make sure Tansy wasn't joking. The purple-haired assistant stood in the doorway, grinning from one rubber-duckie earring to the other.

"Yes. Isn't it exciting?" Tansy gave a little hop, silently clapping her fingertips together. The yellow duckies wobbled. "The bakery wanted more an hour ago. And now the grocery store. Today's edition is selling faster than Ms. Bea's hot doughnuts."

Laurel allowed a jiggle of excitement. It was just one edition, but they hadn't experienced good sales in weeks, so they were allowed to celebrate a little.

"Call the other places and see if they need more."

"Great idea. And then I'm going to the Bea Sweet for celebratory cinnamon rolls."

As Tansy disappeared around the wall, Laurel returned her attention to the computer screen, whispering, "Thank you, Lord."

A reprieve, albeit a small one. She began scanning the newswires, hoping to come up with another engaging story for tomorrow's paper. Heroes and their dogs apparently sold well.

Suddenly, Tansy was back. "Laurel."

"More good news?" She glanced up to find Tansy standing halfway in and halfway out of her office. She was staring toward the front of the building at something Laurel couldn't see.

She was no longer hopping or grinning.

"I think you'd better come out here."

"Why?" Laurel left her desk and stepped over to the doorway. "What's going on?"

Tansy raised a pointing finger. "That."

Through the plate-glass windows where she could watch the activities of Main Street, Laurel spotted Yates Trudeau. A tense, scowling Yates. Her heart jumped into her throat.

As fast as his long legs could carry him, Yates stormed directly toward her, looking as though his brain was on fire.

"Oh no." Laurel stepped out of her office and moved to the counter, thankful it formed a wall between her and the public. Or in this case, Yates Trudeau.

This looked bad. Very bad.

Laurel's gaze fell to the dog at his side. Was he going to let that monster off its leash to attack her? She gripped the silver cross she wore around her neck. Not because she expected it to protect her but as a reminder that God was with her, and even if this mad military hero set his dog on her, she'd be okay. Especially now that Tansy had lofted an industrial-sized stapler in her defense.

"He does not look happy," Laurel muttered.

Tansy emitted a little squeak.

"Maybe he wasn't being modest after all. Maybe he really didn't want to be in the newspaper," Tansy said, right before she barreled inside Laurel's office and slammed the door, taking the stapler with her.

The coward. She'd better not lock that door.

Through the glass, Yates's blue eyes lasered into Laurel's. If a glare could incinerate, she would be ashes.

With one hard wrench, he nearly ripped the handle off the door.

For a man who looked like a good puff of wind would carry him to Kansas, Yates was strong.

Laurel didn't know whether to run or start chucking paper wads, her only available weapons.

She braced herself. Dad had raised her to face problems head-on. A Maxwell neither ran nor cowered.

Her heart, however, ricocheted against her rib cage, faster and faster and faster. If it had legs, it would be far away by now.

Yates came at her, fury emanating from him like heat waves in an Oklahoma August. He slapped today's newspaper on the counter in front of Laurel.

She tried not to jump. She did anyway.

In a voice intended to intimidate, he demanded through clenched teeth, "What. Is. This?"

Oh yeah. Tansy had been wrong. Very wrong. Yates's refusal of an interview definitely had nothing to do with modesty. He *really*, *truly* did not want to be in the newspaper.

Chapter Four

True to his training, Yates mentally clocked details of the newspaper office, though his furious focus remained on Laurel Maxwell. Unlike the Sundown Ranch, the *Times* building hadn't changed a lick. Even the nameplate on the office door still bore Charles Maxwell's name.

The business was oddly silent. Not a soul in sight other than the trim little blonde in a blue skirt and white blouse standing behind the long sales counter. Today her hair was down on her shoulders, curved behind each opal-dotted ear.

She still had a thing for opals.

Head high, posture stiff, cheeks flamed. Laurel Maxwell was not good at hiding her stress.

Something inside Yates reacted, and it had nothing to do with his anger over the unwanted news article. He squelched it.

"I told you no article."

"You said no *interview*. I make the decisions about what to print in this newspaper. And I decided to publish the article anyway."

"You had no right."

"Yes, I did. Freedom of the press is protected by the US Constitution. The very *first* amendment, in case you've forgotten your government class."

She sounded so stiff and pompous he almost laughed. He didn't. He was too fired up. Fact was, he hadn't been this stirred in so long he'd forgotten how it felt. Adrenaline rushes, he knew and experienced on a regular basis. This was something else, something almost enjoyable.

He leaned in until they were nose to nose. Only the wooden counter separated them. She smelled good. Like perfume and doughnuts.

"What about my right to privacy?"

Laurel held her ground. She was no coward. It was one of the things he'd admired about her. She'd always wanted to go public with their relationship, to show their families that Kenos and Trudeaus didn't have to be enemies.

He didn't want to remember that now. Thinking about their past brought back memories he'd rather forget. Memories of a generous, loving, really smart woman whom he'd liked too much. Memories that he couldn't forgive himself for.

But there it was, the ugly thing he'd done. And here he was, blasting her for doing her job.

With a stubborn set to her jaw, Laurel clutched her necklace in a death grip and said, "No amendment directly guarantees privacy as a constitutional right."

Smart aleck. He didn't dare argue with her. She was likely correct. Laurel Maxwell was that intelligent, that knowledgeable.

To his left, Yates detected movement. He slid his eyes toward the office door. Tansy Winchell—Laurel's best friend, who'd known about the secret romance—scowled at him through a barely opened door. A loyal friend, she probably hated him as much as Laurel did.

At his side, Justice stiffened, his hackles rising. He'd spotted the newcomer too.

Yates shifted, his hip and back beginning to protest from his body's tension. He dropped a hand to the dog's pointing ears. Justice eased but remained alert.

He should have left the dog in the truck.

"Are we going to stand here and argue the Constitution or resolve this problem?" Yates kept his tone unfriendly, although strangely enough, some of his rage had seeped out.

"The only problem is your attitude." She yanked the newspaper from the counter and jabbed a finger at his photo, crinkling his face in half. "This edition has already sold more copies than we sold all last week. People are interested in military heroes, especially local ones."

Yates ground his back teeth. "I told you, I'm no hero."

Her chin hitched higher. "That's not what my source said."

He blinked. "Who's your source?"

"I'm not at liberty to say."

Yates huffed a long, annoyed breath that was half growl. They were getting nowhere. "Maybe they lied."

"Did they?" she shot back.

"I don't know. I didn't read the article you were *not* supposed to publish."

Her mouth opened in disbelief. "You're attacking me over an article you haven't even read?"

"This is no attack. If it was, you'd be shredded, and you wouldn't have seen it coming. I'm merely stating my right as a civilian not to be harassed."

She held up both hands, her golden eyes firing missiles at him. "Fine. Consider your complaint received."

"A retraction would be better."

"Not happening. What I wrote is true. No reason for a retraction." She shoved the paper at him. "Read it. If you can prove any of it is a lie, I'll publish your complaint."

He took the paper, noting that her color remained high and her hand trembled the slightest bit. Had he frightened her? Or was she feeling this same weird emotional surge he was experiencing? As if he was alive for the first time in over a year.

Since the moment he'd walked onto Trudeau property

and seen her trespassing, he'd been a mental mess. Now he was amped up like a nuclear reactor. What was happening to him?

Shaking the wrinkle out of the photo of his helmeted head, he leaned against the closest wall and scanned the story. He had to admit, she'd picked a compelling photo. He hated it.

"The story continues on the back page."

That hadn't changed. In fact, everything about the paper, from emphasis on national news to the font size, remained just as Charles Maxwell had left it.

Laurel was nothing if not loyal, another stab in Yates's conscience. She'd been loyal to him too. Against her own family.

So he'd left her.

He flipped the paper over, acutely aware of Laurel's eyes on him. To a woman who'd once fawned over his good looks, he must look pitiful to her now.

Why did that bother him so much?

As he read the well-written piece, his anger dissipated. When she could have skewered him on a flaming spit, Laurel had written a factual, if embarrassingly glowing, report about his military service, his commendations and the blast that had injured him. All public record. Fortunately, whomever she'd spoken with had not revealed his private medical history.

"I like the part about Justice the best," he said grudgingly as he placed the paper back on the counter, this time with much less force.

"I'd be happy to write another article about only the dog."

In spite of himself, he snickered. "You never give up, do you?"

A hint of worry flickered across her heart-shaped face.

"I can't. The *Times* is the Maxwell legacy. I can't be the one to lose it."

So that was it. "Is the paper in trouble?"

"Yes. But that's none of your concern."

No, but you are.

The thought came out of nowhere. Guilt was like that—nearly as stealthy as a recon scout.

He owed her.

He'd also overreacted to the front-page article. The photo in particular had gotten under his skin. He'd dwindled from a strong, confident, robust soldier to a scrawny convalescent who didn't know what to do with himself.

Just then, the heavy front door swooshed open, and a tall woman in a pink pantsuit entered.

Before Yates could take his leave, the woman's gaze fell on him. "Yates Trudeau! It is you, isn't it? The soldier?"

Yates flinched. How had she recognized him? Surely not from the newspaper. He looked nothing like that fierce warrior. "Yes, ma'am. Civilian now."

"I read the article about you in today's paper. It was wonderful. A real hero come home. Seeing you here now must be God's perfect timing."

Oh boy.

When he didn't say anything, Laurel spoke up. "Yates, this is Shannon Prater. She's our regional Big Brothers and Sisters coordinator."

"Ah." What did that have to do with him? "That's… uh…nice."

"Laurel is one of our Big Sisters," the newcomer said, "and I must say, an excellent one. The two little girls she mentors adore her."

Laurel smiled for the first time since he'd entered the building. He'd always liked her smile. "I feel the same about Chelsey and Megan. They're delightful kids."

Chelsey and Megan. The two cute little girls who'd accompanied Laurel's hiking trip. The joyful singer and the purple hat.

"I remember them." Yates lingered out of courtesy for the pink-suited Shannon, who seemed focused on him for some reason. Must be the camo outfit and the untamed beard.

"Which brings me to my reason for being here, Laurel. It's about their dad."

"How is he?"

"Worse, I'm afraid. He wondered if you might be available to spend some extra time with them this week?"

"Of course. I'll run by his house after I close the office and see what works for him."

Shannon put a hand on the arm Laurel had folded atop the counter. "I know this is above and beyond program requirements. You are not expected to act as a babysitter."

"You know my beliefs, Shannon. God put me in those girls' lives for a reason."

The conversation had gone beyond him, so Yates figured it was time to take his leave.

He signaled to Justice and started toward the door. He'd had his say about the newspaper article, even if the outcome was unsatisfactory. And talk of God made him antsy.

Shannon's voice stopped him. "Mr. Trudeau. Yates, wait. Please."

He pivoted. The quick turn stung all the way up his spine.

"Yes?" He knew he was frowning, but the woman couldn't know it was because of the pain, not her request.

"I'd like to talk to you about our program if you have a minute."

"Talk to *me*?" He pressed a finger to his chest.

"Yes. Would you be interested in mentoring a boy? We have a number of single moms in this area requesting a strong male role model in their sons' lives."

Strong? Role model? The only term that applied to him in that sentence was "male."

"I don't think so." He'd been a big brother for real, and look how badly that had turned out.

"You're exactly the kind of man young boys look up to. A soldier, a warrior—and with a military dog to boot." She tapped the newspaper still spread on the counter. "According to this article, you're a real-life hero."

He wished people would stop saying that. He shot Laurel a glare. "Don't believe everything you read."

"Well, you think about it." Shannon handed him a business card. "Why not attend one of our meetings before you say no?"

Hadn't he already said no? People in this town didn't seem to understand that word very well.

The woman turned her attention to Laurel. "Talk soon, Laurel. Thank you for being so kind to those precious girls. They really need someone right now."

Which aroused Yates's curiosity. What was the deal with the girls and their dad?

Not his business.

He was not mentor material.

With a final goodbye, Shannon took her leave.

Time for him to do the same.

"You really should think about it," Laurel said before he could escape. "You could make such a difference in a boy's life."

Right now, he was dead weight on the world.

When he said nothing, she kept going. "With your outdoor expertise, you'd be a natural to introduce a boy to fishing, hiking, nature—all God's wonders. And you practically raised your younger brothers and cousin. You know how to be a big brother better than anyone I know."

"Not completely true, but thanks."

He recognized a compliment—and maybe an olive

branch—when one was offered. But her comment only brought to mind the one brother who'd never made it to adulthood.

Trent had only been fourteen when he was killed. Yates had been the oldest, the guardian who hadn't been on guard.

"Why are you suddenly being nice to me?" he asked.

"I'm always nice."

They both laughed. Imagine that. Her laughing with him. After the way he'd treated her.

"Maybe I was too hard on you about the article."

Laurel sniffed, her color still high, but her eyes sparkling with a different kind of fire. "You were."

He tilted his head to the side, one eyebrow elevated. "Still spunky?"

"Spunkier." She leaned across the counter. "My Little Sisters have an eight-year-old brother. His dad isn't able to spend much time with him anymore."

Her floral fragrance wrapped around his head, swamped him with pleasant memories. "What's the deal with the dad?"

"Diabetes and some sort of kidney disease. I don't pry but I know he's on dialysis and sick most of the time. Their mom died in a freak work accident several years ago."

"Sad deal."

"That's why the Big Brothers and Sisters program is so important. They need you, Yates. Why not attend a meeting and then decide?"

He wasn't doing much else. Basically, he was useless. To the ranch, to himself, to everyone.

He stroked a hand over his whiskery jaw, heard the scrape and scratch.

An excuse to be outdoors and to be there for some kid the way he wasn't there for his late brother appealed to him. Maybe he could make a difference again, the way he had in the army.

Maybe.

And maybe agreeing to something Laurel deemed important could somehow make up for all the ways he'd wronged her.

The newspaper woman was starting to sucker him in, in more ways than one. Not that he'd tell a soul about the strange, zinging, *alive* feelings their conversation had caused. Let sleeping dogs lie and all that. He was sure she'd agree.

They weren't a couple. They weren't friends. She didn't even like him.

"I'll think about it." He held up a finger. "On one condition."

"What's that?"

He allowed the tiniest grin to sneak up the corners of his mouth. "If you promise not to print any more gushy articles about me."

"'Gushy'? 'Gushy'!" Laurel perched a hand on one hip, wishing she'd pressed her skirt this morning, and faked umbrage at Yates's suggestion that anything about the article was personal.

His small tilt of a smile lifted higher. "Gushy."

Laurel fought a snort.

She couldn't believe she was having a friendly conversation with this man.

Had she entered some alternative universe? The kind she'd longed for eight years ago, when he'd suddenly disappeared from her life and she'd prayed and prayed to hear from him? To hear his laughter, to feel his arms around her? To at least know he was okay?

A shiver ran through her. She would not let herself revert to that awful memory.

Yet she liked sparring with him, and she didn't want to. She wanted to whack him upside the head. Except she didn't.

They'd always had such fun bantering and joking about the silliest things.

Ugh. Yates Trudeau had a troublesome effect on her even now, after all the hurt he'd left behind. Underneath the straggly beard and thinner face lurked the same humor, the same cowboy charm messing with her mind.

She should toss him out the door on his bone head.

But any soldier who looked the way he did deserved respect and appreciation. She'd researched the job of an army recon scout. It was scary dangerous. Yates had been in harm's way every moment.

He'd been through a lot that he wasn't talking about. Neither were his superiors. All of which spiked her curiosity to red-alert level.

Gran would have a fit if she knew the two of them were having a semi-friendly conversation. In fact, a fit was on the way as soon as she read today's newspaper. Gran wouldn't care that Yates had been badly injured. She wouldn't care about his service to the country. She'd only care about that stupid Keno-Trudeau feud.

The office door opened, and Tansy, the coward, crept out, still wielding the giant stapler.

Yates flicked a glance in her direction.

"There are no explosives," he said, his tone dry but his eyes lit with humor. "My dog checked. You're safe. For now."

Laurel snickered. Tansy shot her a look that suggested Laurel was losing her mind.

She didn't have to worry about that. Laurel had learned her lesson about getting involved with a Trudeau, especially this one.

He pointed a bony finger at her. "No more news articles."

She held up a stop-sign palm. "Done."

Dog leash rustling against his camo pants, Yates dipped a short nod and headed out the door.

Aware that she was breathing too fast and that her heart was drilling a hole in her chest, Laurel watched him cross the wide sidewalk. Something about his gait was off.

"Do you think he moves oddly?" she asked without taking her eyes off the man.

Tansy bellied up next to her to look. She clunked the heavy stapler onto the counter. "I noticed that. Not a limp exactly, but something."

Yates opened the door to his truck. The beautiful dog hopped inside with one easy, graceful leap. Yates tossed the leash in behind him, reached for the overhead handle and pulled himself into the driver's seat.

The dog moved with much more ease than his master.

"My thoughts exactly. Not a limp, but something off-kilter, as if his spine isn't straight anymore."

"Can that happen?" Tansy asked.

"I have no idea. His superior said he'd been hurt. Yates admitted he had surgery. Neither wanted to discuss the extent of the injuries."

Through the glass, she saw Yates's thin shoulders rise and fall as if he were sighing. Then his eyes captured hers above the steering wheel.

She couldn't look away. "He's in pain."

Tansy bumped her shoulder with her own. "Don't go there, Laurel."

The touch broke the spell, and Laurel rotated away from the haunted eyes of Yates Trudeau. "What are you talking about?"

"I saw the way you got all blushy and flustered."

"'Blushy'? Is this word in the thesaurus?"

"You know what I mean. In between the fireworks, the two of you were practically flirting."

Was that true? It couldn't be. She couldn't allow it.

Laurel put both hands to her hot cheeks. "Don't be ridiculous!"

"I'm not. And now you're watching him as if you feel sorry for him."

"I do. Sort of. Did you notice how thin he is?"

"Not your concern. You're already caring for your grandmother, mentoring two little girls and spending extra time with your Sunday school class."

She loved doing those things. "Your point being?"

"Your natural inclination is to nurture people. Even me and the rest of our staff. And we love you for it. But you can't take care of the whole world. Certainly not Yates Trudeau."

"I wouldn't dream of trying." Yates had family to look after him, if he'd let them. She suspected he wouldn't. He was proud like that. Or had been.

"I'm your BFF, remember? I read you like the front-page headlines. You're concerned about him, and I'm worried you might still care about him." Tansy growled and practically spit out the words. "*Him* of all people. I wish I'd whacked him with the stapler."

"He'd probably have fallen over." Laurel refused to entertain the thought that she might still carry some smidgen of feeling for the man.

"Yes, and then the dog would have attacked me."

"But it's such a pretty dog to get attacked by."

The conversation had become so silly they both chuckled and bumped shoulders.

Still, in the back of her head, Laurel fretted. Asking Yates to be a mentor to Chelsey and Megan's brother put her on dangerous ground.

Yet the need was there.

She couldn't allow her confused feelings for Yates to keep a little boy from having the opportunity to fish and hunt and do man things.

Could she?

Why was she worrying? Yates had said he'd "think about it," which was a euphemism for "not happening."

Laurel pointed to Tansy's desk. "Get back to work before I forget about nurturing and fire you."

Tansy feigned insult. She shouldered her reporter satchel. "I'm going to go find us a news story. When I come back, I'm bringing chocolate. You need it."

After the confrontation with Yates, she certainly did.

As Tansy reached the front door, she paused. "Stop thinking about Yates, Laurel. I mean it. You know what he's capable of."

Laurel swallowed hard.

She did indeed.

After going back into her office, she shut the door, turned today's front-page picture upside down on her desk and forced Yates out of her mind.

If only he'd stay there.

Chapter Five

Yates couldn't get Laurel off his mind. Why had he stormed into the *Times* like the beaches of Normandy and made a big deal out of the news story? It was done. Couldn't be undone.

But he knew why. Ego. Pride.

When he'd stopped at the grocery store this morning to pick up dog food, every eye in the place had stared at him. Even those who knew him by name couldn't cover their shock. The newspaper photo had set him up. People expected a vigorous warrior. They'd gotten him.

It was humiliating.

He'd been better off living in his RV in Centerville, where no one had known him.

Then there was the little thing about seeing Laurel. She brought back a time he'd traveled thousands of miles to escape. Her, Trent, the entire disaster. He should have kept his distance.

No doubt, she felt the same. For her, Yates Trudeau was nothing but a bad memory.

He had no business ever darkening her path again.

Now some pink-suited lady had planted a seed in his head that kept sprouting up like dandelions in the front yard. Laurel had seconded the motion.

But a mentor to a little boy? Him? In the shape he was in? What kid would admire a scrawny, worn-out former soldier?

The dad was sick. Sad deal. Tragic, really. Yates understood about not being able to do certain things that had once been second nature. Like riding a horse.

Some part of his messed-up brain wanted to pray. Imagine that. When he knew prayer was useless. God didn't care.

Yates aimed his truck toward Centerville.

He had some thinking to do. Alone.

Three hours later, his cell phone pinged. Wade wanted to know if he was lost.

His brother didn't know the half of it.

Yates replied, giving his whereabouts—something he was unaccustomed to doing. A recon scout didn't announce his location if he planned to stay alive. But, he thought with a regretful sigh, he was no longer a scout. He wasn't much of anything.

Like everything else in his upturned life, he'd have to make the adjustment.

Assimilating back into his old life would take time.

The army had given him purpose. When he went on assignment, he had one clear goal in mind.

Now his only goal was to heal his body, something he had no control over.

He liked being in control. This wind-sock-in-a-hurricane feeling drove him up the wall.

Back in his truck, he left Centerville and headed to the ranch and the fences he'd forgotten to inspect.

By the time he'd driven the ranch's perimeter and returned to the house, his hip twinged every few seconds and he was tired to the bone. Ridiculous, but true.

As he entered the house, the smell of cooked food made his belly growl. Was he actually hungry?

He unsnapped Justice's leash and hung it on a hook just inside the door. The dog shook out his fur and, after receiving permission, ambled away.

Before Yates could follow his nose, Wade appeared in the entry. "We gave up and started dinner without you."

"Sorry. Got distracted. The fences took a while."

Wade studied him. Yates was pretty sure his brother could read his unnatural fatigue. Was he angry again because Yates had pulled an unintentional disappearing act all afternoon?

Wade's head bobbed. "Are you okay?"

Emotion, that wretched thing, welled in Yates's chest. "Yeah. Thanks. For everything."

"Like what?"

Yates removed his cap. "Being here."

"Where else would I be?"

"You know what I mean."

Wade clapped him on the shoulder. "Yeah. I do. I'm glad you're home. Stop worrying. We'll figure out the rest."

Yates offered a short nod, his throat too thick. Again.

He was the oldest. He should be reassuring his brothers, not vice versa.

"Let's get you fed before Bowie and Sage eat it all." Wade grinned.

Sage. Yates had completely forgotten about Bowie's company tonight. Another mark against him.

Following his brother, he entered the dining room, where his growing family were spread out around the long table. After an awkward greeting and introductions to Sage's niece and nephew, he washed up at the kitchen sink before taking his place.

They'd left his old seat open at the head of the table. Dad's place. Then his.

The frog of emotion rose in his throat again. He cleared it.

Kyra, as pretty as a daisy in May, passed him a warm casserole dish. "Chicken spaghetti. I hope you like it. It's one of Wade's favorites."

"She spoils me." Wade winked at his wife, the love in his expression obvious.

Yates was glad, really glad, that his brother had found true love.

"Sage brought bread from the bakery. She made it. It's amazing." Bowie pushed a plate of slices toward him. Another man who'd found the right woman.

Sage smiled in Yates's direction. "Oddly enough, Yates, I found my true calling in bread dough at the Bea Sweet Bakery."

Sage Walker, a baker. Now *there* was a paradigm shift.

In high school, she'd been all about avoiding carbs and becoming a fashion model, and she had the face and figure to make it happen. With long, nearly black hair; green eyes; and Amazonian height, Sage was even more stunning in maturity.

He wondered what had happened to her dreams, why she was back in Sundown Valley, working in a bakery.

Yates bit into the bread slice and nodded. "Good. Really good."

The response seemed sufficient.

"She brought pastries for dessert too," Bowie said, pointing his fork at Yates's belly. "She'll fatten you up."

"You, too, if you're not careful." Wade aimed the shot at Bowie. The two men laughed. Sage and Kyra smiled at each other.

When he'd left to join the military, the dinner table had been somber. Only the three young Trudeau men had gathered here, all with broken hearts and too much guilty anger, unable to help each other through the worst time of their lives.

Now the family dining table was filled with two loving couples and five children, the three smallest smearing food on their high chair trays and the other two occasionally whispering to each other. One of the triplets had a spaghetti noodle stuck to his cheek.

The scene was happy, restful. Family together.

It was good.

Chest clogged with feelings he didn't know what to do with, Yates filled his plate, letting the conversation move on without him. He was an observer. It was what he did. What he'd once done better than anyone on Earth.

As Yates dug into the creamy casserole, Sage's nephew, Ryder, with his brown hair fighting to stick up in a rooster tail, asked him, "Are you a real soldier?"

"I was."

"Cool. I want to be a soldier when I grow up."

Bowie laughed. His fork clattered against his plate. "What happened to being a cowboy?"

"I'll be that too. He's both. Aren't you, Mr. Yates?"

"I was."

If the answer was vague, no one seemed to notice.

Sage handed the boy a napkin, signaling for him to wipe away a smear of cheese. "Being a soldier is a worthy calling, Ryder, but you have plenty of time to decide."

"Yeah, I guess. Paisley might not want to be a soldier. She likes girl stuff better. I can't go without her."

"Girls can be soldiers too," Kyra said.

"I don't want to," the big-eyed child said from her spot beside Bowie. "I want to bake pies like Aunt Sage."

"I second that." Bowie bent down and kissed the top of Paisley's head. "More pies. Less danger."

"Speaking of soldiers," Kyra said, "what happened in your conversation with Laurel Maxwell about the article?"

All three Trudeau men turned their heads toward Kyra.

"You didn't go to her office, did you, Yates?" Wade said. "She's Keno kin."

As if he needed a reminder.

"I thought it was a really good article." Sage dabbed at her lips with a napkin. "The bakery was all abuzz."

Just what he didn't want.

"I talked to her."

Yates thought Wade might suffer whiplash. That's how quickly his brother's head swung toward him. "That wasn't smart. She'll probably write something else about you tomorrow, blasting you as a quarrelsome Trudeau."

"She won't."

Irritation flashed through Wade's eyes like blue lightning. "Don't go trusting her. You haven't been gone that long."

"Laurel's okay. It's her grandma who's a Keno, not her. They're barely kin to our troublesome neighbors."

None of them knew that he was the bad egg in the conversation, not Laurel.

Time to deflect and redirect before Wade blew a gasket, so he said the first thing that entered his head.

"A woman came in the news office while I was there. Asked me to join the Big Brother program." He made a derisive sound. "Can you imagine?"

Kyra pushed a bowl of green beans toward him. "I think that's a wonderful idea."

"Me too." Sage glanced down at her niece and nephew. "Not all kids have extended families."

There was that. No one knew about being without relatives in her life better than Sage, who'd grown up in foster care.

There was also the issue of Laurel.

Somehow, some way, he had to make up for the hurt he'd caused her. Not only in the past but also today when he'd selfishly blown up at her over a newspaper article. He hadn't considered her—just himself. Like before.

For once, he desperately wanted to do something right when it came to Laurel Maxwell.

Maybe the Big Brother program was a start.

* * *

Two weeks later, Yates walked into an informational meeting of the Big Brothers and Sisters organization. His new Wranglers felt stiff, but the old ones hung on him like he was a kid wearing his dad's clothing. The old boots that Wade had packed away in plastic bins with his other belongings felt pretty good, though.

He stood in the doorway for a moment, getting his bearings, scouting out the lay of the land. By force of habit, he scanned the doors and windows—escape routes—and internalized the places someone could hide.

The meeting room of the Centerville Public Library contained a few round folding tables, the chairs occupied by a handful of people in his age range. Not many, and most were women.

His gaze landed on one particular woman. He hadn't known Laurel would be here and wondered why she was, even as his chest heated in a peculiar manner.

She was talking to Shannon, the woman he'd met at the *Times*' office. Looking professional—and a little too appealing—in a yellow skirt and navy polka-dotted blouse, Laurel didn't notice him.

Careful to avoid the sting of sudden movement, Yates eased into a chair at the closest table.

He felt awkward and out of place, like he had made a mistake in coming. Yates studied the backs of his hands and contemplated a quiet departure.

A soft floral fragrance drifted close.

He lifted his head, experienced a jolt.

"I hoped you'd come." Laurel's welcome tingled the skin on his arms. "Mind if I sit here?"

"No." Why would she want to?

Yates clattered out of his chair and held hers the way Dad had taught him. His movements were frustratingly clumsy and too fast for his hip and spine.

Laurel tilted her head up toward him. "You didn't have to do that. But thank you."

He gave a brief nod as he gingerly returned to the seat across from her. More carefully this time, he straightened his left leg under the table as far as he could.

"You deserve respect, Laurel."

She folded her hands atop the white plastic table, expression earnest. "Do I?"

"Yes."

Their gazes held for several long moments. A beat of time passed.

They both knew they were discussing more than manners.

"Thank you for that. I always wondered if—" She bit her bottom lip and glanced toward the front of the room. "Shannon's about to begin."

In other words, leave the past alone.

Yates wasn't sure he could.

When he owed a debt, he paid it. The problem was, he didn't know how. He also didn't know if she'd let him close enough to repay anything.

Common sense said for her to run for the hills and avoid so much as a glance at him.

Yet she was here, sitting across the white table as cordial as an old friend.

That was Laurel—eternally kind, even to the lowest of the low. Like him. She was a woman who lived her faith.

His was in the sewer, his failures too many.

He could analyze and find a solution to any problem—except his own.

Something seized up inside him, a need strong enough to make him tremble. A longing to turn back time and be the man he should have been. For her. For his family.

But that was impossible. Life had no do-overs.

The meeting commenced, and Yates turned his attention

to a slideshow of Littles and Bigs, as Shannon had termed the program's participants. She explained the mountain of required paperwork, the time involved and a slew of particulars Yates filed away.

Laurel scribbled on a notepad as if she'd never been to a meeting.

Occasionally, she leaned toward him across the table and clarified something Shannon said. Her fragrance circled through his brain, muddling his best intentions.

He was joining the program to make amends, not to mess up her life again.

When the meeting ended, he shoved a pile of handouts into the supplied folder and asked, "You're already in the program. What made you attend?"

"Shannon asked me to write an article for the paper. Recruitment is down. The program needs more adults. Especially men."

Ah. She hadn't come because he might be here.

Good. Good. That was for the best, wasn't it? Then why did his ego sting a little?

Because he was a selfish idiot of the first order.

Laurel rose from her chair and tossed the notepad into a yellow tote. She was about to leave. He wasn't ready to let her go.

He tried fighting the urge but gave up and asked, "Want to grab some coffee or something?"

Yates saw her hesitancy and couldn't blame her. Why have a longer conversation with a jerk like him?

"I thought you could tell me about the boy," he went on, needing her to say yes. "Chelsey and Megan's brother."

Hesitancy fled as her wary expression softened. "Well, sure. I guess I can do that."

Kids, clearly, were her soft spot. Hadn't they always been?

Centerville wasn't a big city, but it dwarfed Sundown Valley. No one in this town knew either of them. No one would give a second glance to a businesswoman talking to a nicely dressed, if somewhat shaggy-haired, man at a small diner.

It had always been this way with their relationship. Side-street cafes. Out-of-town dates. Clandestine meetings. Anywhere to avoid Keno or Trudeau eyes.

Neither of them had wanted to face the firing squad such a discovery would bring.

As soon as the thought came, Laurel reprimanded herself. She and Yates did not have a relationship. Now or in the past. What she'd thought was love had not been enough.

She was a little angry at herself for letting her thoughts go there and even more annoyed that she'd agreed to meet with him in the first place.

What on earth had come over her? And why couldn't she demand answers, blast him with some well-chosen words and never speak to him again?

But they were both mature adults now, civil and polite to the point of painful, pretending all was well when it wasn't. Grin and bear it. The way of the world.

Lord, there must be a reason you brought him back into my life. But why? I want to do the right thing, but this is hard. I loved him so much, and he hurt me so badly.

While she stewed, the waitress took their orders for coffee, talking them into slices of homemade pie in the process.

Yates could use the calories.

No, she was not nurturing him. She was observing and stating facts. That's what a journalist did. The man was too thin.

"How are you, Yates?"

Ugh. There she went. Tansy's nurturer accusation practically screamed in her head. Yet her faith meant treating people the way she wanted to be treated. Even if Yates hadn't.

But that was years ago. He was clearly not the same person he'd been back then.

"I mean, truly, how are you? How are you adjusting to civilian life? How is your recovery going?"

He studied her as if questioning her sincerity. "Off the record or on?"

Of all the things for him to ask. "Off. I told you I wouldn't write anything else without your permission."

Yates nodded. "I'm okay."

She snorted. "It is obvious to anyone with sight that you are not—" she raised her fingers in air quotes "—okay."

"I'm getting there. What about you?"

The question caught her off guard. He wasn't supposed to be nice. He was supposed to be the creep who'd left her without a word so she could despise him.

Lord, what are you trying to teach me here?

"I'm fine." She should tell him about Aiden and leave.

His fingers tapped the table between them. "Worrying over the newspaper?"

Really? He was asking about the paper? Who did that? Who went away for eight years without contact, then waltzed back into her life and behaved as if he cared about the things that concerned her?

"The immediacy of the internet and twenty-four-hour television reports has really hurt the newspaper business."

Such a civil conversation when the undercurrents screamed for attention. She wouldn't let them out. Couldn't.

Talking about the paper was more comfortable than asking why—or worse, asking if he'd ever really loved her or if she'd been, as Tansy had suggested, a pawn in the Trudeau-Keno game of chess.

"Newspapers do a more thorough job," he said.

"I think so too. No sound bites. No half-truths and quick memes. We lay out all the facts and let people decide for themselves." She shrugged. "But most people don't want to slow down and read today. They prefer the quick and easy, even if it's not thorough."

The server returned with two saucers of warm peach pie, each dotted with a scoop of melting vanilla ice cream, followed by cups of fragrant, fresh coffee.

She didn't need the calories, even if he did. She took a bite anyway and hummed her approval.

Yates, she noted, didn't touch his.

Instead, he took a sip from his pottery mug and scanned the room over its rim. She had a feeling he could describe everyone in the café—what they wore and even what they ordered. He'd also, she'd noted, taken a seat facing the entry with his back to the wall.

Though he appeared relaxed, she suspected he wasn't at all. In his job as an army scout, he couldn't let down his guard for a moment. All the stress he must have been under. She understood ordinary stress, but for him, lives had been at stake.

There she went again, feeling empathy for him.

All the while, her head kept asking the same questions: Why had he left the way he did? Why hadn't he contacted her? What had she done wrong? And why couldn't she stop blaming herself when he was the bad guy?

Setting his cup aside, Yates spoke without meeting her eyes. "I'm sorry about your dad."

She blinked in surprise. Was he sincere? "Even if he was half-Keno?"

She probably shouldn't have said that. Yet it had always been a barrier between them, the one obstacle they hadn't overcome. At least, she'd *thought* her family was the issue. Had she been wrong?

Yates didn't take the bait. "The two of you were close."

"Losing Dad was the hardest thing ever." Harder even than losing Yates. Dad hadn't left on purpose. "But you know about the loss of parents. Yours died so young. At least I had Dad into adulthood. He was my anchor."

She had no memory of her mother, who'd died of a rare illness shortly after Laurel's birth. Dad had raised her with Gran's live-in help.

"I still have Gran," she went on. "She's nearly eighty-three now, and her heart is bad, but she's as feisty and contrary as ever."

Neither Dad nor Gran would have approved of Laurel's romance with Yates if they'd known, but the Kenos' animosity toward the Trudeau family wasn't to blame for the way things ended.

Yates was.

So why was she here with him?

Because she was a journalist. She needed to know. Yates had always been a complicated—if charming—man, as deep as Sunset Canyon.

She wasn't here tonight because she still cared for him. Nor was she inclined to take care of him, no matter what Tansy said.

She was just…curious. And determined to find a Big Brother for Aiden. Yates would be a good one whether she liked him or not. If it took sacrificing her feelings in order for a child to feel important, she was willing.

Jesus expected no less than her best, especially when children were involved.

Using the side of his fork, Yates sliced off a bite of pie and pushed it around the saucer. The ice cream created white swirls in the golden peach juice. "So you inherited the *Times*."

"Yes."

"As I recall, that wasn't your plan."

He knew her dreams. She'd once told him everything. She'd thought he'd done the same. He hadn't.

Still, he'd remembered, and his remark was salve to a bruised place on her heart.

"That's true," she said. "I thought I wanted to work for a major news outlet in the city, and I did for a few years. But Dad had always intended that I would take over for him someday. When he suffered a sudden, massive coronary four years ago, well—" she lifted both hands in a shrug "—I took over."

"Are you happy?"

It was such a strange thing for Yates, of all people, to ask that she didn't know what to say for several long seconds.

Happy? In what way? She had a good life. Her faith and friends sustained her. Even if she sometimes felt as if something was missing.

"Dad spent his entire adulthood building the best newspaper in this county. He entrusted that legacy to me. I'd be foolish not to appreciate it."

"Same for me and the ranch, I guess."

"But you left." She waved away the comment. "Sorry. Let's not go there." They were having a strangely pleasant, civil conversation. For Aiden's sake, Laurel refused to introduce a sour note. "We're here to discuss Aiden."

His eyebrows lifted. "Aiden?"

"Chelsey and Megan's brother. Shannon is confident she can match the two of you once all your paperwork clears—if that's what you want."

"Tell me about him. About all of this Big Brother stuff."

She pointed. "After you taste that pie. It's delicious. Maybe as good as the bakery's, but don't tell Ms. Bea."

He offered an almost smile before taking a man-size bite.

"Well?" she asked.

He chewed thoughtfully, as if judging a contest. Some of

the old Yates humor danced in his bluer-than-was-prudent eyes.

After swallowing, he said, "I'd need a slice of bakery pie before I can choose. It's been a while."

Charmer. Teaser. She'd once thought him to be the finest man on earth.

Though he was familiar in too many ways, she didn't really know who he was anymore.

Did she even want to?

She shouldn't, but even after all these years, she yearned to better understand what had happened between the two of them.

Tansy's voice practically screamed in her ear. *Don't be a fool.*

Tansy was convinced Yates had only dated Laurel in some perverse scheme to prove he could. Laurel hadn't believed it. Until he'd left.

Then she'd just been hurt and confused. And worried.

From the looks of him, she'd been justified in the worry.

With the uncomfortable, unspoken past hovering between them like a thick fog, she whipped out her phone and steered her thoughts elsewhere.

"I have a photo of Aiden." She scrolled through the picture app. "Occasionally he tags along with the girls and me. We take lots of selfies. It makes the kids laugh."

"You feel bad leaving him behind."

He still knew her too well.

Had she ever known him at all?

"That's where you come in. He's all boy. Outside, kick the ball, run, jump and climb. The sort of thing the girls and I don't enjoy much."

She pushed her cell phone across the table to him.

"Handsome kid."

"All three of those kids are pretty. They're good kids, too, Yates. Aiden won't give you any problems."

"Worried I can't handle him if he does?"

"Not at all. But I want you to enjoy him, the way I enjoy the girls."

"You were always a kid magnet."

"You know how I feel about children. They're so delightfully open and candid and hilarious. They look at the world with fresh eyes."

"I wouldn't know."

"You'll learn fast now that you're home with five little ones running all over the ranch. You'll probably add a couple yourself in a few years."

Something in his easy demeanor fled. His jaw tightened, relaxed. He pushed the pie plate away.

"Not happening," he said easily, but with enough steel to be deadly serious. "No kids for this old cowboy."

"But what about your wife? I mean, when you find someone to put up with you." She laughed a little at the end to show she was teasing.

He wasn't.

Expression solemn, he stared out the window at the parking lot.

In a quiet, almost-aching voice, he said, "No wife. No kids. I'm not the marrying kind, Laurel."

No one knew that better than Laurel. So why had she kept digging until he'd disappointed her? Yates was not the man for her. Never had been, never would be.

She was furious that it bothered her.

But it still did.

Chapter Six

During the following weeks of enduring fingerprints, a background check, a home study and other social services intrusions, Yates worked toward adjusting to his new situation.

To regain his strength, he hiked, fished, wandered the wilderness alone and made himself as useful as possible around the ranch. As long as it didn't require heavy lifting, he fed stock, mucked out a stall or two before his energy faded and drove his truck into town for various supplies.

Whenever he drove past the newspaper office, he'd slow down. He wanted to stop, but he had no excuse to go inside. Besides, if he entered the *Times* building, word would drift back to Laurel's grandma, and she would have to deal with the repercussions.

He didn't doubt the newspaper article had caused a heated conversation or two between the women.

He wanted to make amends to Laurel, not cause her more trouble.

Other than the Big Brother program, which wasn't directly for her, he hadn't figured out a good way to do that.

She'd treated him politely and with unmerited kindness, but he could feel the wall she'd erected against him. Not that he blamed her.

He parked next to the loading dock at Youngblood's Feedstore and went inside the only farm store in Sundown Valley. The sweet molasses scent of livestock feed greeted him as he approached the sales counter and handed over his handwritten list.

After the clerk rang up the purchase, Yates wandered around the small farm store while he waited, taking in the interesting odds and ends a person could find only here. Toward the back, baby chickens peeped and pecked in an open bin warmed by an overhead light.

Yates reached in and gently lifted a fuzzy yellow chick, stroking the top of its head until it closed its eyes, peacefully trusting.

Would the triplets enjoy raising baby chicks? Or were they too small yet to be gentle?

He'd have to ask.

He had an affinity for animals. Always did have. He'd missed this interaction with nature. God's creation, as Laurel would call it.

He wished he still shared her faith, wished that trusting was that easy. How did a man find his way back to a God he didn't trust anymore?

"Trudeau."

The harshly spoken word caused him to turn away from the warm chicken bins.

His belly clenched.

Short, thick legs spread in a belligerent stance, a rotund, ruddy-faced man sneered at him.

Yates exhaled an inward sigh. "Bud Keno."

Of all the people to encounter, he had to meet the neighboring rancher who'd caused issues for the Trudeaus for as long as he'd lived. What had begun years ago in some sort of feud had reached warlike proportions when father and son, Bud and Bill Keno, had taken over the Keno ranch. They savored trouble.

"Saw that newspaper article," Bud said. "Treating you like some big shot hero. I don't know what's wrong with that girl, but she's gonna hear from me about it."

Taking a second to get his temper under control, Yates

turned away and carefully eased the soft chick back into his flock.

"Don't turn your back on me, Trudeau. You aren't that important, though your bunch of horse thieves think they are."

"Leave Laurel and the paper out of this. She's only doing her job."

"Laurel, is it? Just like before you ran off to the army?"

When Yates didn't say anything, Bud laughed an ugly laugh. "Oh, the two of you weren't as clever as you thought. I've been hiding that knowledge in my back pocket for eight years, just itching to use it."

An arctic chill ran through Yates. "You don't know anything. As I said, leave Laurel out of it."

"What would that cocky brother of yours do if I gave him a call? Kick you out? Hate your lousy guts? He wouldn't cotton much to his brother romancing a Keno woman." An ugly smile slit Bud's fat cheeks.

Yates clenched and unclenched his fists. Anger stirred under his rib cage.

How could this man be related, even distantly, to a fine woman like Laurel?

And exactly what did he know about the romance Yates and Laurel had worked hard to keep secret?

From somewhere in the distance, a disembodied voice called out, "Feed's loaded, Mr. Trudeau."

Yates lifted a hand in response to the clerk's call, though he kept his focus on Keno.

Did this guy know Yates could dispatch him with his bare hands in less than five seconds if he wanted to? Even in his damaged condition?

But his fighting days were over. He wanted peace.

"Isn't it time we all grow up and stop this senseless quarrel? I don't even know how this started. Let it end here and now, Bud. Become good neighbors, if not friends." The last word nearly choked him.

"You'd like that, wouldn't you? Sweep the truth under the rug and hope I forget that I'm in the driver's seat."

The knot in Yates's stomach tightened to the point of pain. "I'm warning you, Bud. Back off."

"Or what?"

Yates stepped close enough to smell the coffee on Keno's breath. "You *know* what. Eight years in military hot zones taught me the tools to get it done this time."

Something flickered in the other man's pale irises, an awareness akin to fear.

While he had the upper hand, Yates turned and walked away.

He didn't like using that kind of threat. He wasn't a rowdy young man with a quick temper and faster fists anymore.

But Bud Keno didn't know that.

Truck loaded with ranching supplies, Yates followed the winding gravel roads between the small town and Sundown Ranch.

Some days it was as if he'd never left. Others, he felt like a complete stranger. He wondered if it was like this for all military personnel as they reacclimated to civilian life.

Probably not. They hadn't left behind the kind of mess he had. The kind of mess that still lingered like the smell of a cow lot.

Rolling down the window of his truck, he let the fresh air blow through while he revisited the unpleasant encounter with Laurel's distant cousin.

He hadn't known anyone was aware that he and Laurel were a couple back then. If not for that one horrific day, he wouldn't care now if the whole world knew. Fighting over trivial matters didn't interest him anymore. Truth was, no kind of fighting interested him anymore. He was tired of it. Worn slick as a flat rock in an ice storm.

Letting someone hurt people he cared about—well, that

was a different matter. He'd protect his family with his life. Laurel too.

She'd done nothing wrong.

But as he analyzed the conversation, he realized Bud's words had mostly been insinuations. What did he actually know? What proof did he have?

And if he knew something, was he dirty enough to use it against Laurel just to hurt a Trudeau?

Maybe. Probably. Bud enjoyed stirring the pot.

Yates could not let that happen.

Bud Keno was as much an unpredictable loose cannon as ever.

The man liked trouble, seemed to get up each day and run to it the way the Bible said an evil man did.

Yates grunted. How had the Bible gotten into his thoughts?

Listening to devotionals around the dinner table each night, a new thing, must be getting to him.

A long time ago, he would have prayed for a resolution. But what was the point?

Yates sighed, fretting and wrestling the situation for a resolution that didn't come.

He was a problem solver but this one had him stymied.

Or maybe he was anticipating a problem where there wasn't one.

He'd started the day upbeat, full of pancakes Wade had served up with a side of eggs and bacon. His brother had let his wife sleep in while he, Bowie and Yates jostled around in the kitchen like old times.

It was the first meal he'd been able to fully enjoy in a while, a meal without a knot in his chest.

Today was a gorgeous day—warm and humid, the sun out, thunderstorms predicted for tonight. Spring in Oklahoma brought storms but also the rain that grew lush pastures for their stock.

"I kind of like the purge of a storm," he said to Justice,

seated next him in a safety harness. After the unnerving confrontation, he could use a good storm.

Tongue hanging out, Justice smiled as if he agreed, although Yates suspected the thunderous weather would make him jumpy. An explosives dog that had seen too much, Justice suffered PTSD even if his owner didn't.

Pressing the remote to open the gate, Yates pulled his pickup truck down the long driveway toward the ranch house. The remote-controlled gates were another new installment, one he especially appreciated.

Bowie and Wade let him set his own pace around the ranch. He figured Bowie had convinced Wade to leave him be for now. It was the kind of thing his peacemaking cousin would do.

"They probably talk about me when I'm not around," he said to Justice.

The dog adjusted easier, faster than he did. Justice was a sap for Kyra and had decided the three noisy toddlers were okay, if a little unpredictable. Accustomed to constant change, noise and human beings, the dog minded his manners but knew when to duck and take cover.

Trying to put Bud Keno out of his thoughts, Yates parked inside the open bay of barn two and left the truck for someone else to unload. He'd never asked but was grateful that the other men seemed to understand his limitations and his pride without questions.

As he eased out of the truck, followed by Justice, Wade entered the barn. "The other boys will be along soon to unload."

"Thanks."

"Thanks for picking up this stuff. Saved me a trip to town."

Yates wished he'd waited until later. Until Bud Keno was long gone and far away.

"Happy to be useful. I'm not accustomed to doing nothing." Fact was, the inactivity made him a little stir-crazy. He'd started hanging out with the horses more than the people. Grooming, trimming, spraying for flies—he could handle those tasks.

The horses were getting so spoiled they followed him around.

Now he had the creepy feeling that Bud Keno was watching, cameras everywhere to spy on him. He'd keep a lookout.

How could Bud have known about him and Laurel? Why bring it up now after all this time?

Wade opened the tailgate, the metallic sound loud in the enclosed space. The smell of horse feed wafted out. Dusty. Sweet.

"Great breakfast this morning."

"Yeah. Kyra was up with Abby last night. Stuffy nose. I figured I could do KP duty with you two boys."

"Good times." The kitchen camaraderie was like the old days. Except for the missing brother.

Wade paused, one hand braced against the tailgate.

"Right. It was. So don't you think it's time to talk about it?"

Yates stiffened. Talk about what? His thoughts flew to Keno's suspicions.

Please, not that.

Sooner or later, he'd have to discuss Trent and his culpability in the boy's death. But not yet. Not until he found the best way to approach the subject and still maintain a relationship with his one remaining brother.

"What do you mean?"

Bag scraping against the truck's metal bed, Wade shouldered a feed sack with practiced ease.

Like a total slacker, Yates could only watch. He hated that.

"The blast that injured you. The surgery."

A relieved breath seeped out. This he would rather talk about, at least a little. "Six."

"Six what?" A scowl wrinkled Wade's forehead. "Surgeries?"

"Yes." Maybe more to go, but he'd keep that under his ball cap until he knew for sure. No use adding worry.

Wade tossed the feed sack into the store room, dusting his hands as he turned. "Where? What kind? When?"

Yates hesitated, thinking. He'd have to choose his words carefully not to reveal too much, but putting off this talk was only creating more tension with his brother.

"Over the last year and a half. Had some work done on a hip and a leg."

Among other body parts. Talking about the shrapnel and the back surgeries would open the floodgates to more questions he did not want to answer. He'd start with the leg-and-hip issue. The rest he preferred they never knew about.

With a grin he didn't feel, Yates said, "Put it this way, I set off airport alarms."

Wade squinted, his gaze roving up and down Yates's body. "Metal rods, screws, pins, that sort of thing?"

"The whole nine yards." He and the docs joked that he was held together with office supplies—paper clips and staples. Maybe some duct tape.

Joking was the only way to deal with the fact that the slightest shift of residual shrapnel would paralyze him.

Paralyze. A word he didn't even want to think about.

"Man." Wade yanked off his hat and shoved a hand across the top of his head. "Is that why you haven't been on a horse?"

"Something like that. Got a lot more healing to do." If it ever happened. "I want to. I just can't." He tried to joke. "If I undo the docs' good work, they might charge me double."

Wade's powerful hand came down on his shoulder. Expression worried and tender and loving enough to cause a lump in Yates's throat, he said, "Take all the time you need."

Yates narrowed his eyes at his brother in a threatening glare. "Don't go babying me."

"Wouldn't dream of it, you lazy scoundrel. We all know you're playing off to get out of work."

That was better. No pity.

Yates grinned. "You caught me."

"Like when we were kids, and I'd pretend to have a stomachache so I wouldn't have to buck hay in the heat. Dad always knew."

"I did the same. It never worked."

Both men smiled, remembering the good times when their parents were alive.

Talking about Mom and Dad was easy.

The subject of Trent, however, was forbidden. As much as he hated Wade thinking that Yates blamed him for the tragedy, the real truth was worse. Twofold.

He didn't want to lose the only brother he had left by purging his guilt. Neither did he want to hurt Laurel any more than he already had. He had kept her name out of it then. No reason for that to change.

"Text me when my truck is unloaded. I'm driving to Centerville later to bring my RV home." He gestured toward the back of the truck. "Sorry I can't help."

Wade snorted. "No, you're not. Lazy dog." To the actual canine, he said, "Sorry, Justice. No insult intended. My brother's the slacker."

Yates's chest filled. Wade, for all his porcupine quills, was a better brother than he'd ever been, intuitively understanding Yates's need to hold on to the scrap of pride he had left.

He turned to leave, heading for the house and one of those health drinks Kyra had stocked for him. She didn't think he ate enough. She hadn't seen the pile of pancakes he'd devoured this morning.

Sweet woman. She cared about everyone. No wonder his brother loved her so much.

Wade's voice caught up to him. "Hey, Yates."

Yates glanced back in question.

"I love you, man. And I'm praying. All of us are. When

you're ready to tell me everything else that's eating a hole in you, I'm here."

With a quick nod, Yates turned away and kept walking, fighting the moisture that sprang to his eyes and the heaviness in his heart.

"Line one, Laurel," Myra barked from the layout room. "I wish someone else in this place would learn how to answer a phone."

Tansy looked up from her desk and wiggled her eyebrows.

Laurel grinned and reached for the black receiver. Myra was in one of her moods today. The rest of the crew ignored her bluster and kept working.

"*Sundown Valley Times*. Laurel Maxwell speaking."

"Laurel, Shannon Prater with Big Brothers and Sisters. How are you?"

Frantically trying to plug the leak in the newspaper dam, she thought, but only said, "Great. Yourself?"

They went through the required niceties and then Shannon got to the point.

"The reason for my call is good news. Yates Trudeau has been approved as a Big Brother for Aiden Stafford. We did a video chat with him and Aiden's dad, who also approved the mentorship."

"That's nice. I'm happy for Aiden." What did Yates's approval have to do with her?

"But there's a problem."

"Oh?" Had something in Yates's background check proved less than stellar?

"Aiden is eager to get started, as you can imagine an eight-year-old would be when he learned his Big is a former soldier with a retired military dog."

Laurel smiled, imagining the little boy's excitement as she pinched a bite of chocolate frosting from Tansy's latest bakery gift.

"He plays army a lot and *craves* a dog," she said. "I don't think I've ever seen him without a toy soldier in his pocket."

"Here's the issue. The best time for them to get together is tomorrow, but I can't get to Sundown Valley to make the introductions. Since you know all involved parties, I need a favor. Will you meet with them this first time to break the ice?"

For over a week, Laurel had managed not to think about the troublesome Trudeau. Now here he was, right back.

Refusing Shannon's request wouldn't make sense. Laurel was the one who'd urged Yates to become a Big. Aiden needed him. And if she wasn't mistaken, Yates needed this too.

No, she was not nurturing her ex-boyfriend.

It was an introduction, not a date. She was not getting involved with Yates again. He'd made that perfectly clear.

The meeting would be on neutral territory at the Stafford home. Gran wouldn't know. Laurel wouldn't have to listen to another lecture like the one she'd received for publishing Yates's article.

What else could she do but agree?

Yates had trouble sleeping Friday night, and that was out of character. He might not eat well, but he was a great sleeper. Had learned to sleep anywhere, any time.

But not last night.

As if he didn't have enough on his mind after the encounter with Keno, Shannon of the pink suit had phoned Friday afternoon, asking him to meet Laurel at the home of their three Littles on Saturday.

Exhaling, he rubbed his palms together, releasing some pent-up energy.

He was going to be a Big to an eight-year-old who was "all boy," which could only mean one thing: Aiden rolled, jumped, played sports and otherwise used his body in every physical pursuit known to humans. That's what "all boy" boys did. Yates should know. He and his brothers had been "all boy."

He had an exhilarating memory of jumping out of the barn loft, among other wild and dangerous stunts he and his brothers had pulled.

Had he made a mistake in agreeing to this? Would he be a big disappointment? Or cause himself more injury than he could afford?

How would he keep up with a rambunctious eight-year-old?

With a growl, Yates paced the floor of his militarily organized bedroom. Before the army, whenever he wrestled a problem, he'd ride his horse fast and far until he'd arrived at a solution.

He couldn't even do that anymore.

The last time he'd ridden the wind had been the night he decided to join the military. To leave his home, his family and Laurel.

He hadn't been on a horse since.

Then there was also the problem of encountering Laurel again.

He hadn't expected her to be involved, though now that he thought about it, he should have known she would be. He was mentoring the brother to her Little Sisters.

Shannon couldn't be present today. Laurel knew the kids. End of subject.

If his stomach dipped to think about seeing Laurel again, he figured it was guilt. Anxiety. Some negative emotion associated with all the messes he'd made.

Though he lived out in the country, Sundown Valley was a small town. They were bound to see each other now and then.

Be polite. Complete the mission. Get out.

"Thirteen-hundred hours," he said to the dog watching him with golden eyes. "Want to go meet some people today?"

Justice's tail thwacked the tightly tucked covers of the guest room bed. Yates's bed for now.

He had contemplated living in his RV, now parked behind the house, but when he'd mentioned it, his family had objected. So he stayed. Being in the house, surrounded by memories and family, was getting easier. Maybe the contact was good for him.

Like Kyra's protein shakes.

Bowie was building a beautiful home for himself and Sage near Sunset Canyon, but until the wedding next summer, his cousin occupied his old room. Yates supposed he, too, could build, but why bother? He'd never have a wife and kids the way Bowie planned.

"This guest room or the RV is good enough for us, isn't that right, buddy?"

A guy who'd slept on the ground more often than in a bed wasn't that picky.

Except he still felt like an interloper.

Here in the ranch house, though, the lively triplets entertained him and the dog on a regular basis. They were hilarious little scoundrels.

Where were they, anyway? They usually banged on his door and demanded his attention. Sometimes he let them in, though he was frustrated that he was unable to lift them and roughhouse when they reached for him.

Even as he enjoyed their cuteness, they reminded him that he'd never be a dad. He'd never know the exuberant love of a child.

"No use crying about it, Trudeau. God gives and He takes away." He choked on the remainder of the paraphrased verse: *Blessed be the name of the Lord.*

Seemed as if God had done more taking in Yates's life than giving. How could a man bless that?

He checked his watch. "0700."

He had plenty of time before meeting Laurel. Rather, Aiden. Laurel wasn't supposed to be his focus. The boy was.

But she occupied his thoughts anyway.

To distract himself, he tapped the watch face and

stroked his fingers over the wide leather band he'd worn all over the world. Bowie, his artistic cousin, had created identical watch bands for all of them. A labor of love, a connection between the four Trudeau males.

Trent had been buried with his, though the glass face had been shattered.

Slamming the file drawer on *that* thought so fast his ears rang, Yates studied his face in the mirror hanging over the dresser. His cheeks had filled out some, but he still needed the beard to cover the bones and hollows.

The curly brown whiskers were long and a tad messy. More than a tad. Straggly, according to Wade.

He'd frightened the little girls that day near Hidden Pond. Would they be scared of him today?

He stroked a hand down the coarse beard. When had he last shaved? Before the blast?

Wouldn't hurt to get a trim. Maybe a haircut.

"The barber'll need a chain saw."

Yeah, he'd go into town early, trim the beard and hair, try to look more presentable.

For the little girls, not because of Laurel.

He wondered why she'd agreed to meet him there. Why was she being nice to him? Why didn't she just skewer him and be done with it?

Considering his future physical condition, it was best if she disliked him anyway.

Chapter Seven

Tag was a harder game than she remembered.

Trying to work off the unsettled nerves that spiked every time she thought of encountering Yates again, Laurel chased Aiden around the front yard of the Stafford home. Whenever she stretched out a hand to tag him, the slippery boy dodged and took off in a new direction, laughter spilling out like rainbow sugar sprinkles.

The girls ran in wide circles around her, yelling in a singsong tune, "Na-na-na-na-na. Laurel can't catch me."

At four and six, they were easy catches, but she pretended to miss a few times.

Suddenly, Chelsey stopped in her tracks and pointed. "Look! Miss Laurel. Bigfoot."

Laurel's heart jumped into her throat. Bigfoot could only mean one person: Yates.

He slammed out of his pickup truck, dog at his side, and ambled toward them in his off-kilter gait. It bothered her, that gait. Yates had always been athletic, graceful, moving with lithe cowboy ease she'd found particularly attractive.

He was more injured than he let on.

She wondered if he'd tell her the details—not that they were her business. Not personally, anyway.

Why had she agreed to make this introduction? Was she that much of a martyr?

But she'd prayed about it, about him, and being here

felt like the right thing to do. God demanded she forgive, show kindness and mercy. This was a start, she supposed.

She leaned both hands on her knees and waited for him to cross the lawn. He wasn't fast anymore.

The knowledge broke her heart a little. Which was ridiculous. But there it was.

She was a sap.

The kids gathered around her, staring at the newcomer.

"Out of breath?" he asked, amusement in his tone.

"Tag," she said, straightening with one long inhale and exhale.

"I remember you." Four-year-old Megan, cheeks rosy beneath double ponytails now gone askew, pointed a tiny finger at Yates. "You were in the woods. We played with your dog."

"That's right."

"Are you Bigfoot?"

His teeth flashed. He touched his beard. "Do I look like Bigfoot?"

Both girls tilted their heads to one side.

"Not so much anymore," Chelsey said as she fumbled to replace the purple cowgirl hat she wore everywhere but school. "But kinda. I think you might be him."

Laurel laughed. "I think what she's trying to say is that you look different."

His fingers and thumb stroked the outline of his jaw. The scruff made a scratchy sound, sending a weird, unexpected shiver over her skin.

"Trimmed up a little. What do you think?" He directed the question to the girls. "Improvement?"

Chelsey's shoulders lifted in a shrug. "I guess. But it's okay if you're Bigfoot. We'll still be friends. Right, Megan?"

Megan's red bows flopped with her double ponytails as she nodded. "Yep. Jesus says to love the unlovely."

Yates's head went back in a laugh that completely changed his demeanor.

Embarrassed, Laurel laughed with him, then said, "You look nice, Yates. I like the trimmed beard."

The change accented the fact that he was still very good looking. Surrounded by brown hair and beard, his blue eyes stood out like lasers in a dark room.

"At least they aren't scared of me this time." He turned toward the boy, who stood quietly listening. "Hello, Aiden."

"Mr. Trudeau."

Yates offered a hand. "Call me Yates."

Aiden put his small hand in Yates's, and the two shook. An uncomfortable silence followed, as if neither seemed to know what to say.

"So." Laurel clapped her hands together once. "What should we do today? Play board games? Go to the park? Any suggestions? There may be some Little League games happening at the sports complex, if you want to take in a game. We'll go slow and easy today so Yates and Aiden can get to know each other. Okay?"

Yates turned a questioning gaze her way. "I didn't expect you to hang out with us."

"Oh. Well." That hurt. He didn't want her help. "Shannon seemed to think that would be the best way to break the ice. But if you'd rather not—"

"No. I mean, yes. A group thing seems right. I just didn't expect—I didn't want to put you out."

Though her face burned with embarrassment, she managed, "You didn't. This is for Aiden."

Behind the neatly trimmed beard, his face closed up. "Right. For Aiden."

Exactly. They were both here for Aiden. No other reason. They were nothing to each other.

After today, he and the boy would be on their own. She and Yates wouldn't be spending any more time together.

That's the way it was meant to be. So why did it bother her?

Because he was hurt and she was a sap.

Because they'd left so much unresolved.

Because she'd once loved him with every fiber of her being.

Ugh. Sometimes she drove herself up the wall.

Yates signaled toward the front door of the brick house. "You three decide the activity while I go in and speak with Aiden's dad again. Be right back."

The two had met. Parental preapproval was required, but Laurel saw no reason to object. Men had their own way of doing things. Yates, in particular.

That he was here at all amazed her.

Yates expected awkward silence in the truck as he drove the boy to their chosen venue at the city park while Laurel escorted the girls in her car. In the army, silence had been his friend. On scouting assignments, he could go days without talking to anyone. Always thinking, always alert, but silent.

Civilian life was different. People didn't like empty air.

Fortunately, the boy chattered like a chipmunk all the way, inundating him with questions about soldiers and airplanes while alternately telling Yates his life story.

Dad was sick. He couldn't play anymore. That was okay. Aiden loved his dad. Aiden wanted a dog, but Dad said no. He couldn't take care of a dog. But Aiden thought he could. He was glad Yates had a dog. It was really nice of him to hang out. But Dad said he'd got hurt in the war, and so Aiden had to be extra calm and thoughtful.

"Am I being calm and thoughtful, Mr. Yates?"

Yates grinned at the windshield. "Yes."

"Can I touch your dog? Is that calm and thoughtful?"

"Justice will think so. Go ahead. Stick your hand toward the back seat and let him smell you."

Aiden did as he was told. "Does that make us friends?"

A glimpse in the mirror told Yates that Justice was straining forward in eagerness.

"He likes you."

"Yes!" Aiden pumped an arm. "Having a Big is going to be so much fun!"

The exuberance tickled Yates, lifted the dark cloud that seemed to hover around him.

He didn't want his limitations to be a disappointment to the kid.

By the time they arrived at the park—a complex of open fields, playground equipment and a huge wooden kids' play area surrounded by picnic tables—Yates was reasonably confident he and the charming, outgoing boy would get along.

Comrades in arms. Without the arms.

After handing Aiden the leash, he let the boy lead Justice to where the girls were already swarming around a picnic area. Laurel set a small cooler on the concrete table.

She'd thought of drinks and snacks. He hadn't.

Chelsey and Megan fell to their knees in front of the dog and joined Aiden in petting the Malinois.

"Can Justice come in the fort with us?" Chelsey looked up at him, dark eyes lively. She was wearing the purple hat again, and one of her bottom teeth was missing. Cute kid.

Justice's tail fanned the air at the mention of his name. The dog knew how to behave in any situation.

Yates unsnapped him. "Let him decide."

To the kids' delight, Justice chose to follow them to the wooden structure.

Turning her back to the table, Laurel perched on the concrete bench, facing outward to observe the kids. In jean capris and a yellow T-shirt, her blond hair swinging around her shoulders, she was as familiar as his name and prettier than ever.

Not that he should be thinking this way at all.

"Might as well sit." She patted the hard bench. "They'll run around like wild geese for a while, especially with the dog." She smiled up at him. "I'm glad you brought him."

He eased onto the bench, keeping a good four feet between them. "Figured Justice would be a hit even if I wasn't."

Laurel cocked a shapely eyebrow. "Why wouldn't you be?"

His shoulder lifted in a shrug. She knew why. "Sorry Shannon put you on the spot like this. I don't want to cause trouble for you."

She swiveled her knees toward him, expression probing. "I won't play that game anymore, Yates. None of this business about bad blood between our families, if that's what you mean. Do you hear me? I refuse to be the one who continues this madness. It's wrong."

Hadn't he said this very thing when he'd encountered Bud at the feedstore? Lot of good that had done.

He lifted his palms, fingers spread in surrender. "Total agreement."

He was too tired to fight anymore. Over anything.

But the Keno-Trudeau feud wasn't the only reason he should keep his distance. He deserved Laurel's animosity on a personal level. Though she treated him kindly, something he did not merit, there was no way she could have forgotten or forgiven the way he'd left her.

As if she hadn't heard his agreement concerning the trouble between their families, Laurel forged ahead. The woman had a point to make, and make it she would. "We're intelligent adults, free to choose our friends as well as our enemies."

"Which one am I?"

She shot a sassy expression in his direction. "The jury is still in deliberation."

Yates laughed out loud. This was Laurel. "Honest as always."

The way he hadn't been.

Like building blocks, his sins piled higher and higher, driving his guilt deeper. Even now, he was chock-full of secrets.

How could he untangle the messes he'd made without hurting more people. His brother. His cousin. Laurel.

To his relief, Aiden's voice drew his focus toward the play area.

"Look, Yates," Aiden yelled. "I'm way up high."

The eight-year-old hung upside down by his knees on the monkey bars.

"Be careful," Laurel called. To Yates, she said, "He's a daredevil at times. Loves to climb. You'll have to watch out for that."

"Typical boy. We like physical challenges."

"Is that why you agreed to be Aiden's Big? To challenge yourself?"

"Something like that." But mostly to please her, to somehow make amends without revealing everything she didn't know. "I wasn't doing much good for anyone else."

"What about the ranch work? I suspect Wade and Bowie are happy for your help."

"Not yet."

Her amber eyes studied him. He saw when the tumblers fell into place and she understood his meaning. "I see. The injuries."

He dipped his chin in agreement.

"Are you doing physical therapy?"

"Doing most of it at home now. After a year in rehab, I know the drill. But yeah, I drive to the therapist once a week."

He didn't know why he'd added that. Why he'd admitted any of this.

Her eyebrows drew together. "A *year* in rehab?"

"Give or take."

"Oh, Yates." Sympathy, that vicious emotion, crept into her tone. He hated it.

Tone curt, he replied, "I'm fine."

Laurel was too easy to talk to. Always had been. Maybe it was because she was a trained journalist, or maybe it was her innate personality. Either way, he'd always been comfortable talking to her.

He had expected that to change, for her to be colder toward him.

Why wasn't she? Was it her faith? Do unto others and all that?

"Are you being nice to me because I got injured?"

"What do you think?"

"Most of the time, I don't know what to think about anything." Yet his brain never shut off. He gnawed on every little detail the way Justice gnawed on rawhide. "But get one thing clear—I don't want sympathy. I'm still in one piece. That's a big deal."

"Any more surgery in your future?"

"Why do you ask?"

"Just making conversation."

"Let's talk about something else besides me. Boring topic."

"Ah," she said, and that one word let him know that she wasn't fooled.

Laurel swiveled on the hard bench to open the cooler. "Want a Coke?"

If Yates didn't want to discuss his injuries or the obvious promise of more surgeries, that was okay with her. Why she probed could only be laid at the feet of her father, who'd taught her to question and dig beneath the surface.

There were many intriguing layers to Yates Trudeau.

But Dad's advice was supposed to be about newspaper reports, not friends.

Or whatever Yates was.

"No thanks," he said to the offer of soda. "I'm okay."

"That's debatable." She handed him a can of Coke anyway.

He grinned, shaking his head. The Coke fizzed as he popped the top. "How's the newspaper business?"

She opened her soda and sipped the sweet drink.

"Same."

"Still struggling?"

"Afraid so."

"Anything I can do to help?"

She made a face at him. "You've already ruled out more interviews."

Inclining his head in agreement, he said, "There have to be more interesting stories than me."

"Dad built the *Times* and his reputation on hard-hitting news reports. Politics, government corruption, national and world events."

"Maybe people don't want to read that anymore."

"That's the problem." One shoulder lifted in dejection. "They don't."

"Then give them something else."

"Like what?"

"You said the article about me sold well. So maybe people want to read about locals, school and club events, church activities, meetings of the Lions Club. I don't know. Something different, more personal."

She sat up straighter, a tad insulted by the idea. "You can't be serious. The *Times* is my dad's legacy. I can't destroy his dream by changing everything he worked so hard to build."

"What about *your* dreams?"

"Dad's dream is my dream," she replied, hackles rising.

"Is it?"

"Of course it is. I haven't changed a thing about the *Times*."

"How's that working out for you?"

She gave him her coldest glare.

"Publishing articles about the senior citizen bingo games or church suppers, or giving front-page headlines to school field trips doesn't make a good newspaper."

"Why not?"

His questions were starting to annoy her.

"Because it's not hard news." She plunked her drink can on the table and turned her attention toward the playground. "Hey, kids, anyone need a drink?"

All three hot, sweaty kids—followed by a tail-wagging, tongue-lolling Justice—ran to her. She passed the drinks around.

Yates poured water into his cupped hand and let the dog lap. According to the easy way Justice accepted the drink, it was something they'd done before.

When the dog finished, Yates wiped the wet hand down the side of his pants and said, "I was trying to help, not upset you."

She softened. "I know. Thank you. I apologize if I was edgy."

"Understandable. You want to do right by your dad."

"I do. I don't want to disappoint him. My grandma lives to remind me not to destroy the gift he left me."

"You're too smart to let that happen."

He'd always told her how smart and capable she was. She'd loved that about him.

Being here with him, watching him act with kindness toward the dog and the children—toward her—and listening to the timbre of his voice, even when she disagreed with him, eased a hard place in her soul.

They had always been able to talk about their troubles. Or so she'd thought.

For years, she'd longed to answer the phone and hear that manly voice in her ear, to hash out her worries.

She shouldn't feel a yearning toward him anymore, but she did.

Both a dilemma and a pleasure. That was Yates, just as he'd always been.

Only now he was infinitely more interesting.

She was enjoying this time together more than she'd expected. So much so that the rest of the afternoon spun by too quickly.

Yates made every effort to entertain Aiden and get to know him, though he limited his physical activities to tossing the ball back and forth and a low-key game of basketball HORSE.

Aiden didn't seem to notice anything lacking. He clearly had a blast, his admiration for the former soldier apparent. He yelled "Yates, watch this!" a hundred times. Each time, Yates stopped what he was doing to watch and comment.

There was a good man inside that wounded, taciturn body.

Not that she would dare feel sorry for him again.

Laurel had, however, expected an awkward, self-conscious outing. Instead, she and Yates played together with the children and talked as if they'd never been apart.

Like old times. Except for any hint at their romantic past. No touching. No kissing. Definitely not.

Why she would think about any of *that* annoyed her.

The day was for Aiden and the girls, not for revisiting a long-dead romance.

Yet when the appointed time arrived to take the kids home, she struggled against sadness, not wanting the day to end.

And that was dangerous.

Chapter Eight

The next day, when the rest of the Trudeaus headed to church, Yates headed to the horse barn.

The young horses needed work and so did he. Time to move forward.

Anything to get Laurel off his mind.

"Even dreamed about her," he said to Justice with a disgusted huff. "Must be the guilt."

Not to mention the worry over Bud Keno and what he knew or didn't know.

Inside the tack room, he gathered the equipment he needed, looping a bridle and lead rope over one shoulder, the training crop in the other hand.

Since coming home, he'd spent time with these horses every day. They had become comfortable in his company. Now they needed training. He might not be able to ride yet, if ever, but he could lay the groundwork.

Maybe.

So long as the horse cooperated.

As he put the first mare through her paces, his thoughts circled around to his family. They were in church, all of them. From babies and Sage's niece and nephew to the adults.

All but him.

He'd seen the questions in everyone's eyes. Right now, they were offering him a grace period, but Wade wouldn't hold his tongue for long.

Then what? He couldn't afford any more conflict with his brother. But church? The whole painful reminder of how God had failed when it mattered most?

How *he* had failed?

But if sitting through a sermon would make the family happy, shouldn't he do it?

Yates clicked his tongue at the young quarter horse filly trotting easily around the pen. Her ears pricked toward the sound.

Good disposition, clear eyes, beautiful conformation, smooth gait—she'd be a dream to ride.

He fairly itched to throw caution to the wind, toss a saddle on one of the ranch's broke horses and fly across the pasture.

But the first time could also be the last time. Wasn't that what the surgeon had told him? Don't take chances?

Chance had once been his middle name. He'd loved the adrenaline rush of taking risks, both as a cowboy and as a soldier.

What did a man do when he still breathed, walked and talked, but his life had ended?

Laurel's faced popped into his head.

Once, he'd have told her all about the catastrophic injury. Fact was, he had almost blurted the whole story yesterday. But why burden her? He had already done enough damage to her tender heart.

He wondered why she wasn't married.

As much as he fought the feeling, he cared about her. Always had, even when he'd been too young and foolish to recognize her worth.

Why had God taken away his content military life and forced him back to this mess he couldn't untangle?

God again.

His family must be praying for him at church right now. He wished they'd stop.

Except he didn't.

God was powerful. When He wanted to be.

After fifteen minutes, sweat beaded on Yates's face as well as the filly's coat. When she came to a stop, he waited for her in the center of the ring. Head bobbing, bottom lip relaxed, she ambled toward him.

"Enough for the day, Lady Lou." He scratched beneath her chin. "Good job."

After brushing the horse down, he turned her out to pasture and leaned on the metal corral railing to watch her join the herd.

Thirsty and annoyingly fatigued, he started back to the house, Justice at his side.

His phone chirped. A text from Wade indicated the family was going out to eat after church. Did he want to meet them at the restaurant?

He typed his reply, feeling lonely, feeling apart. Infuriatingly, he was too tired to go anywhere, but he cleaned up and drove into town anyway.

When he arrived, the after-church crowd packed the Sunday buffet at Sundown Family Restaurant. Noisy conversation and the scent of fried chicken greeted Yates as he wove through the tables to where his family waited.

He'd barely sat down when Paisley, Sage's doe-eyed niece, said, "Finally! Let's pray. I'm hungry."

Chuckling, they bowed their heads while Bowie offered a simple prayer of thanks.

Thanks for what? Yates thought. Yet the easy way his family embraced their faith stirred him and caused a longing in his chest he didn't want.

In a clatter of chairs and plates, they joined the buffet line. Yates's appetite was slowly returning, and the roast beef tempted him.

Wade sidled up and plunked a golden piece of fried chicken onto his plate. "Eat."

The chicken smelled really good. Hot and fresh. Yates grinned, giving his head a shake. His brother was taking care of him.

As he started back to the table, he spotted blond hair. His grin fell away.

Laurel. Across the room. Enjoying Sunday dinner.

And she wasn't alone. Or with her grandma.

Stephen Stafford—with Aiden, Chelsey and Megan—sat with her around the square table. They were talking, laughing.

A thought hit Yates like a fist.

Was Laurel romantically involved with Aiden's dad?

He hadn't expected that. But why not? They were close in age. They both cared about Stephen's kids.

Yates got a funny feeling in the pit of his stomach.

He ate his meal in silence, his appetite gone. No surprise there. It had nothing to do with Laurel.

"The carrot cake here is amazing." Kyra, sitting to his right, leaned closer. "You should try it."

"How did you know I like carrot cake?"

"I'm married to your brother."

He speared Wade with a mock glare. "Talking about me?"

His brother snorted. "You're so endlessly fascinating."

"Carrot cake is tempting." He hadn't had the spicy cake in a long time.

"Loaded with cream cheese frosting." Kyra was determined to feed him. "Go."

Not wanting to hurt her feelings, he headed to the dessert bar.

As he pursued the offerings, someone bumped him from the side. He'd started to scoot over when a familiar voice said, "I see you eyeing that carrot cake. It's fabulous. They make it fresh on-site."

He looked up to find Laurel standing next to him, white dessert dish in hand. "Is that what you're having?"

"Nope. Ice cream with lots of hot fudge. Maybe a chocolate chip cookie or two."

"Tempting. What about your date?" He winced. Why had he asked that? He wasn't jealous. She wasn't his anymore.

Laurel's eyebrows dipped. "My date?"

She glanced back toward her table. "Oh, you mean Stephen? We're just friends."

He'd heard that line before.

"I thought he was too sick to do anything."

"Today is one of his better days. He wanted to buy my dinner after church as a thank-you. A real kindness, considering all he's going through. What could I say except yes?"

She and Stephen attended church together. Faith had always been at Laurel's center. It was one of the things they'd shared. Once.

Yates took a plate of the carrot cake from the bar, aware that his stomach was rolling too much to eat it but not knowing what else to do without looking stupid.

"Nice of him." As if his legs wouldn't work—a terrifying thought—Yates remained next to her. "Aren't you worried about talking to me in public?"

She pointed a finger at his nose. "I told you. That's over."

He wished someone would tell Wade. And her grandma. And all the other Kenos.

"In fact," she said, "I came to the dessert bar not to overindulge in ice cream but because you were here."

"Really?" He wasn't quite sure he believed her. He didn't deserve her friendliness.

"Yes. The kids had such fun yesterday. They asked if we could do it again, all of us."

All of them? "Even the dad?"

He liked the guy, but having him along seemed weird for some reason.

"No, silly. Stephen's not up to more than a sit-down dinner. I meant you, me, the kids. They saw you over here and urged me to ask."

"You'd do that? Go out with me?" Heat crept up the back of his neck. Poor choice of words. "I didn't mean… What I meant was—"

"I know what you meant." She glared at him again, and he thought she might jab him with a fork. "I would. I will. We aren't a couple. But we can be friends. For the sake of these kids."

Right. The kids.

She'd endure his company for the children.

A few days later, Laurel arrived home after work to find Gran puttering in the flower garden.

Today had been another day of worry, another reminder that she might not be able to save Dad's newspaper business.

Yates's ideas had entered her thoughts more than once, but she ignored them. Dad would roll over in his grave if she turned the *Times* into the town's gossip rag.

But what would he think if she had to close the doors?

What would she do with her life? Move back to the city? But what about this white-haired woman who'd given up so much to raise her only grandchild?

"You look spritely this evening," she said to Gran.

Leaning back on her knees between the pansies and the daisies, Gran patted the portable oxygen bag. "Feeling like I'm twenty."

Laurel smiled. "I'm going out after I change."

Gran's eyebrows shot up. "Got a date?"

Laurel's pulse jumped. Guilt, she figured, not anticipation. "Sort of. I'm taking the kids to a baseball game at the school."

Gran scoffed. "That's not a date."

Exactly the reminder Laurel needed. This was not a date. Yates had made that very clear. "Will you be okay here by yourself?"

Gran waved a trowel. "I'm old, but I don't need a babysitter. Go on. But spruce up and wear some color, for pity's sake. I heard one of the coaches is single."

Laurel laughed and shook her head. If Gran knew who she was meeting at the Stafford home, she wouldn't be so jolly.

Heading inside to get ready, her pulse fluttered to think about spending an evening with Yates. Date or not, they'd be together, like old times. Except this meeting was in public, out in the open.

The town would wonder, gossip, make them a couple. It was what small towns did.

Tomorrow at work, Tansy would question her sanity. Rightly so.

But try as she might to forget about Yates, she couldn't.

Something pressured her to reach out to him. Was it the Lord? Did He expect her to go the extra mile for a wounded warrior?

She latched on to this explanation.

She would face the explosion with Gran when and if the time came.

She was tired of fretting about what other people thought, tired of letting the past rule her future.

Except it did, especially where Yates was concerned.

She didn't want to care, didn't want to get her heart involved.

But he was broken and she was a fixer.

Showing kindness to a wounded warrior did not equal falling in love.

Digging in her jewelry case, she found a pair of opal earrings Yates had given her for Christmas one year. She hadn't worn them since he'd left. She hadn't thrown them away either.

Leaning toward the mirror, she slid the small jewels into her earlobes.

"Father God," she murmured, "am I off base here? Are you the one orchestrating these meetings, urging me to reach out to him?"

She wallowed the question in her head, aware that God worked in ways she'd never understand.

"Yates needs You, Lord. I know You love him as much as You do me. And he is troubled, Your specialty. I want to do Your will, whatever that might be. If it's spending time with him, help me not to fall in love again. My heart can't take it."

The home health nurse was in the Stafford living room when Laurel arrived. So was Yates. And the two seemed to be enjoying themselves.

An uncomfortable disturbance pinched beneath Laurel's sternum.

Wasn't the nurse supposed to be here for Stephen? Why was she in the living room, chatting up Yates?

"How's Stephen?" Laurel asked, proud that her voice didn't betray her ridiculous jealousy.

The nurse, a slim brunette with trendy glasses, glanced toward the closed bedroom door. "He's not had a good day. Yates tells me you're taking the children to a ball game. Thank you. Mr. Stafford needs the rest."

"Happy to help."

The nurse put a hand on her arm. "He talks about you all the time, about how you've made a difference to his kids."

Laurel felt Yates watching her. Did he really think she and Stephen were a couple? "I'm sorry we can't do more."

"No one can." The nurse gathered her bag and notes. "Except God."

"Is he getting worse?"

The nurse looked to be sure that the children were otherwise occupied before replying. "Yes."

The bottom fell out of Laurel's stomach.

All the way to the sports complex at Sundown Valley School, she wrestled the meaning of the nurse's words.

What would happen to these kids if Stephen could no longer care for them?

She longed to hash out the worry with Yates. He'd always been a problem solver. But she wouldn't broach the topic tonight. Not in front of the children.

Fans packed the bleachers surrounding the lighted baseball field, even though the weather hinted at rain.

As Yates purchased tickets and led the way through the gates, a few old friends paused to say hello. Most mentioned the newspaper article and he winced, aware that his current rail-thin form did not match the picture. In his short weeks back, he'd put on a few pounds but not enough.

He managed to dodge questions about his injury and was grateful when Laurel looped her arm through his and said, "We should find a seat while we can. The stands are filling up fast."

He gazed down at her, felt the connection between her sweater-covered arm and his. Something turned over inside him. "Like old times."

In more ways than one.

To the talkative man and woman, he said, "Good seeing you."

Relieved to escape more scrutiny, he let Laurel and the three children lead him toward the bleachers.

As much as he'd prefer an empty private seat, out of curiosity's view, Laurel laughingly led them up the steps, excusing her way through a sea of tightly squeezed bodies to an empty spot on the third row. Right smack dab in the middle of the metal bleachers.

The woman really did not care that half the people in the complex were watching them.

His admiration for her shot up another notch.

She was one tough cookie. Strong in ways she hadn't been before. Incredibly appealing and sporty in roll-cuffed jeans and a hot pink hoodie, with her ponytail poking out the back of an Eagles' ball cap.

He loved the way she looked.

Just as the PA system squealed to life and began announcing the starting players, Yates settled beside her, leaving as much space as possible between them. In seconds, he was scooted closer by more people crowding onto the bench.

Aiden sat on his left. The girls sat on Laurel's right. As if this was a conspiracy to push the two adults together in the center.

Why fight it? He was here. And Laurel smelled really good.

Leaning toward Aiden, he asked, "Do you play in the Little League?"

"Not this year. I used to, though, when Daddy was better."

Heartbreaking.

"Must be tough for you and your dad."

"Yeah. But it's okay. Daddy says he'll feel better some day and we'll catch up."

Yates hoped that was true and admired the dad for trying to encourage his son.

"So you know baseball rules?"

"Oh yeah. I played second base. I'm fast and can catch the ball. You have to know the rules to play second." He squirmed in the seat to angle his body toward Yates. "Did you play ball?"

"I did. Baseball, football, basketball, ran a little track." He'd rodeoed, too, but stopped after Trent died. Angry bulls turned his stomach.

The game commenced, and Yates listened to Aiden's chatter while increasingly aware that Laurel's side was crushed against his.

They'd have more room if he slipped his arm around her waist.

He wouldn't though.

Word was bound to get back to both their families anyway. He could handle his. But he didn't want Laurel to have to deal with her grandma or Bud Keno. No use pouring gasoline on a pile of explosives.

She leaned toward him, stirring her flowery scent and good memories. "The girls and I want hot dogs. Want one?"

"I'll get them." Yates stood, eager to escape thoughts of Laurel's soft fragrance and softer skin before he said or did something they'd both regret. "Want to go with me, Aiden?"

"Sure." The boy gazed around the crowded stadium and then said to Laurel, "Save our place, okay?"

"I will arm wrestle anyone who tries to steal it."

Aiden frowned. "Can you win?"

She flexed a nonexistent muscle. "What do you think?"

The boy looked up at Yates and grinned. "I think we'll have to find another place to sit."

While Laurel snorted, pretending to be insulted, Yates laughed.

Laughing with Laurel felt good.

Everything about her company felt good.

He patted the boy on the shoulder. "Come on, buddy. Dogs and sodas."

"Candy and popcorn?" the boy asked hopefully.

"We'll talk about it."

Grinning, they wove through the crowd and down the steps. Steps weren't his friend, but Yates refused to hold the rail, refused to give in to the tweak in his hip and lower back.

Three steps. He could handle those. *Take each one easy. Don't lose your balance.*

He, who'd jumped out of airplanes onto unknown terrain, now worried about a mere six-foot tumble.

When they reached the ground and started toward the concessions, Yates forced himself not to limp. Not with the small admiring boy stuck to his side like a wood tick and a stadium full of townspeople looking on.

Joining the long line winding toward the snack bar, they waited their turn. Yates spoke to a few acquaintances. Occasionally, a roar or a groan rose from the stands. He squinted toward the place where Laurel and the girls waited.

His phone chirped with a text. One plain dog. Ketchup on two.

She still liked her hot dogs plain. He smiled and shot back a reply. Hope you're not too hungry. Long line.

We're patient. Wow, did you see that catch?

How could I in this sea of people?

You're tall.

Not that tall.

Sorry. Her text was followed by laughing emojis.

They kept up a back-and-forth while the line crept ever closer and Aiden talked to a buddy from school.

Yates and the boy missed the bottom half of the fourth inning but finally got their order and had started back through the crowd when the one person Yates didn't want to see blocked his path.

"Excuse me." Hands full of hot dogs, Yates tried to step around Bud Keno, who must have come to watch his grandsons play.

"Not so fast, big shot," Keno said. "Didn't I warn you to stay away from Laurel Maxwell?"

"Neither of us is your business, Bud. She's barely even in your family tree." Yates started around him again, but the rotund Keno stepped in front.

"I got something to say." An ugly grin creased the man's red face. "Something you don't know."

"I'm with a young friend here, Bud." Yates dipped his chin toward Aiden, who watched the two men with wide eyes. "Don't make a scene."

To the boy, Yates said, "Take those drinks to the girls, Aiden. I'll be there in a minute."

Reluctantly, Aiden did as he was told but kept turning his head to look back.

When the boy was out of earshot, Yates focused his attention on the belligerent neighbor. He was tired in so many ways, and this was one of the most exhausting.

"Whatever you have to say can wait. I came to watch the game."

"Then you better get back to it, pal. I know something you don't, but I'll let you fret about it awhile. It's a real doozy. I'm sure your brother would find it…painfully interesting." Bud laughed that ugly sound again. "Enjoy your hot dog."

Chapter Nine

For the rest of the evening, Yates stewed over Keno's comments. What was he getting at? Nothing good, for sure. Did he really know something harmful to the Trudeaus? Or was he bluffing to make Yates worry? Would he really do or say something to cause problems for Laurel just to dig at the Trudeau clan?

Laurel was the worry plaguing Yates. He didn't want anyone causing trouble for her, especially now, when he was permanently back in Sundown Valley and trying to make amends for the past.

Twice during the next few innings, Laurel mentioned how quiet he'd become. After her third comment, he tried to put the encounter with Bud Keno out of his mind and focus on Aiden. And her.

She was fun, no doubt about it. How could he have forgotten?

Her wit and warmth drew him in. When the home team fell behind two runs, she led the girls in waving their rally towels and yelling, "Rally, rally, rally!"

He'd cheered with her when the next batter hit a three-run double, and she jabbed him with her elbow and yelled, "We did it. We rallied the troops!"

Except for Bud Keno, tonight had been amazing.

Because of one feisty woman who refused to give up.

After they dropped the children off for the night, Yates walked Laurel to her car and opened the door.

The dome light came on, blending with the porch light Stephen had left burning for the children.

Laurel touched his arm. "Thank you for tonight. I know you didn't want to come."

She was wrong. That was the dilemma.

He allowed a small smile. "I didn't hate it."

She laughed. "I'll take that as progress."

"Aiden's a sweet kid."

"He is. You're making a big difference for him too. According to his dad, you call every day after school to ask how his day went. Thank you."

Yates leaned his forearm on the top of the car door. His back screamed from sitting in the backless stands. "I like him."

And her. He liked her. Still.

Very bad idea.

"Yes, but he was starting to act out at school." She tilted her head, smile wry in the dim light. "That is, until you told him that a soldier shows respect and follows rules if he wants to stay alive."

Yates huffed a short laugh. "I didn't say the last part."

She waved it away. "Eight-year-old interpretation. The point is, Aiden admires you. You've helped him. And his dad."

Her appreciation made him feel better about his other failures. "No big deal."

"It is to them." Her hand slid from his forearm to his fingers. She squeezed the tops of them. "And to me."

Her touch was like a soothing balm. He craved it.

With her face tilted toward him and the porch light shining through the shadows, he could see the glow in her eyes.

Unless he missed the signals, she still cared about him.

He cared about her too. Always had. Even when he'd been too young and angry to know it. Even when he'd failed her.

What he felt couldn't be love, exactly. He dare not go there. Yet he could not deny that the emotion swirling in his chest was deeper and more satisfying than friendship.

Laurel's lips curved softly as their gazes held.

Way deeper.

She was so pretty. So...special.

Emotion shifted beneath Yates's rib cage. His pulse kicked up. His brain shorted out.

Ignoring the alarm bells clanging in the back of his brain, he lowered his head and kissed her. Just a short, sweet thank-you kiss, but it rocked his world. What he really wanted to do was snug her up close and make up for lost time.

Foolish. Maybe a little nuts. But there it was.

Laurel took a step back, expression quizzical. "How's your spiritual life, Yates?"

Yates blinked five times while his brain recalculated. How had they gone from kissing to *that*?

"Excuse me?"

"You used to share your faith easily, but after Trent's death—"

His whole body stiffened. "We're not discussing Trent."

He cut her off before she could say more, but the damage was done. A bucket of ice water down his back wouldn't have chilled him any worse.

"Exactly," she said, with part annoyance and part concern. "Maybe you *need* to talk about it or whatever burden you carry on your shoulders like a five-hundred-pound weight."

He turned to one side, stared at the house next door. The moon reflected off the chimney flashing. "I should go."

A beat of silence passed between them that spoke volumes. Why did everyone want him to talk about things that hurt too much to remember? Some things he could never talk about. Ever.

He'd carried hundred-pound packs for days without help. He could carry this.

Burdening others with his personal terror was selfish. He'd rather stay bottled up and carry this heavy load to his grave than to upset either her, Wade or Bowie ever again.

What they didn't know literally would not hurt them.

"Goodnight, Laurel." He started toward his truck, but Laurel's small hand, like a powerful magnet to iron, caught his arm.

He glanced back at her.

"Why did you leave the way you did?" The words throbbed from her throat, telling the tale of how much sorrow he had caused her. "Without a word? One day you're here and then I never hear from you again."

Guilt flooded in, a tidal wave. He really didn't know why he'd shut himself off from everyone he cared about. Selfish. Cruel. Afraid of losing his courage. Afraid if she objected, he'd never be able to leave her behind. And he'd had to go. He'd had to get away.

"I thought it was best at the time."

"Best for who?"

He removed his ball cap, put it back on. "I was so messed up back then, Laurel, after Trent died. No excuse, no reason, no explanation can ever be enough. I'm sorry."

He pulled up short from telling her the whole story. Purging his conscience would only make her feel responsible. He might feel better. She wouldn't.

"You're quiet this morning."

Laurel looked up from the article she'd read three times. She still didn't know what it said. The memory of Yates's sweet kiss wouldn't go away.

Why had he kissed her? And why had he resisted a discussion of his faith? He'd been angry and confused after Trent's death, but had he given up on God altogether?

Faith was her bedrock. She couldn't navigate this life without Jesus.

No wonder Yates was troubled.

"I'm thinking," she muttered in response to Tansy, who lingered at the door to her office, coffee cup in hand.

"About Yates?" Tansy asked. "I heard you were with him last night at the game."

Laurel had known this was coming. She'd felt the tension from Tansy from the moment the assistant editor had entered the *Times* building without her usual offering of sweets from the Bea Sweet Bakery.

"No, Tansy," she said, "I'm not thinking about Yates. I'm trying to come up with a reason not to fire you."

"You're blushing." Tansy stepped inside the office and pulled the door shut. "Everybody's talking about the two of you. Speculation runs rife."

"Everybody? A rather broad generalization, isn't it? The mayor was in here ten minutes ago to discuss the agenda for the next council meeting. Therefore, not *everyone* is talking about me. Your comment is hyperbole at best, silly at worst."

Tansy pointed the coffee cup, a mug emblazoned with the words *I'll probably spill this*. "Oh, you are good. Sidestep, redirect, avoid the topic. You should be in politics."

"Right now, I'm in the newspaper business, and if you want a paycheck, go back to your desk and work."

"Cranky. Again. That man has a strange effect on you."

"It's not him. It's this paper."

"So he's not making you cranky. He's making you blush. Does your grandma know yet that you've been out on the town with the enemy?"

"He is not my enemy."

"He should be."

"No, he shouldn't. I don't *want* enemies." She *wanted* Yates to kiss her again. The errant, but truthful, thought deepened the blush on her cheeks. "Jesus intended us to get along, to forgive, to give people a second chance. And yes, Gran had heard by the time I got home last night."

"Did she need an extra heart pill?"

"Probably. I didn't ask. I explained that Yates and I are going to be seeing each other because of the Stafford children. She'll have to deal with it."

"I doubt she was happy."

"No, but I was. Telling her was a relief."

"She's afraid for you, Laurel. So am I."

"Couldn't my best friend trust me a little in this?" Her head was starting to throb. "Please."

"I just want you to know I have your back."

"Then let me talk to you about Yates without constantly reminding me that he jilted me. You and Gran hurt me as much as he did with your reminders that I'm not enough for any guy to fall in love with."

Tansy sucked in a roomful of newsprint-scented air. "Laurel, I never meant that at all."

Laurel leaned her elbows on the desk. "That's the way you made me feel."

"I am so sorry." Tansy plunked her cup on the edge of the desk, splattering drops of coffee, and came around for a hug. "I was only trying to protect you. Forgive me?"

"If you'll return to being the friend who cheers me on instead of beating a dead horse."

"I will. Scouts honor." She slapped a hand over her heart. "And to prove my exceptional love for you, I'm going next door for Bavarian creams. A peace offering. A token of affection. Be right back."

During the weeks that followed, Yates put Bud Keno as far back in the recesses of his brain as he could hide them. His head was too full of other things.

Somehow Laurel had forgiven him and seemed to want

him back in her life, at least as a friend—which had to be enough, all things considered.

Her kindness was a stunning concept to his over-guilty conscience. He refused, however, to question it. Laurel was letting him make amends in the only ways he knew how.

Of course, she didn't know everything. That's what haunted him, popping up like an evil jack-in-the-box when he least expected it.

As Bigs to the Stafford Littles, he and Laurel spent a considerable amount of time together. Granted, the kids were always present and served as strong reminders to keep the relationship on the friendship chart.

But he couldn't resist the pleasure of an occasional friendly goodnight kiss after dropping the kids off for the day.

Falling in love was not in his future. Couldn't be.

He'd reconciled himself to growing old alone.

Which put him in a confrontational mood this particular evening after a day in Laurel's sweet company.

If friendship with Laurel was all he could allow, he intended to enjoy it without recriminations from his family.

Ambling down the ranch house hall, he stepped into the office.

Wade looked up from his laptop. "You look better."

Yates gave a short laugh. "Than what? The roadkill that showed up here a while back?"

"Yep. That. I'm glad to see it."

"Glad to feel it." He patted his belly. "Being home is packing the pounds on me."

"You've still got a ways to go."

In more ways than one.

Taking hold of the wooden chair arms, he eased himself down. His cranky lower back whined. "We need to talk."

Wade pushed the laptop aside. "Okay. Shoot."

"Where's Bowie?"

Wade's eyebrows shot up. "That serious?"

"I hope not."

Wade tapped out a message on his cell phone. "He went to the horse barn to check on that mare in foal."

Yates could have done that. He still wasn't much help on the ranch, but the horses had always been his domain.

Wade propped both elbows on the desk and steepled his fingers together. "Want to tell me what this is about?"

"I'll wait for Bowie." He'd barely finished the sentence when his cousin loped inside, breathless.

"What's up? Trouble?"

Wade waved a hand at Yates. "Ask him."

Yates's pulse thrummed against his collarbone. His chest felt tight.

"No trouble unless the two of you make it."

Bowie and Wade exchanged glances. "Okaaay."

Gripping the chair arms in a strangle hold, Yates blew out an anxious breath.

"I'm seeing Laurel Maxwell. Strictly the Big Brother and Sister program, but we're spending time together, and I don't want any backlash about it. Especially to her. My life. My decision."

Silence filled the room while his declaration sank in.

Finally, Wade said, "That's not smart, brother."

"Why not? Because of some stupid conflict between you and Bud Keno?"

"Between all of us and the Kenos."

"Which you continue to perpetuate." He'd been gone eight years. This wasn't his fight anymore.

Wade's jaw flexed, his eyes hard. "Him. Not me."

"Whoa." Bowie finally opened his mouth. Yates and Wade hushed. Their cousin was like the famous advertisement: when he spoke, the rest of them listened.

Removing his hat, Bowie turned it upside down on the

edge of the desk and quietly spoke to Wade. "Let Yates tell us what's going on."

Wade folded his arms and sat back in his roller chair. "Okay. Shoot."

Stumbling to find the right words, he told them about Aiden, about the sick dad and the natural way the Big Sister and Brother program had created a friendship between him and Laurel.

"So that's why you've gone into town so much lately."

"I'm surprised you haven't heard. We haven't exactly kept it a secret." He winced at the latter, recalling the original secret romance with Laurel that none of his family knew about. The secret romance that had cost Trent his life.

"Laurel *is* a fine Christian woman," Bowie said. "She does good for the town, and she's never caused us a problem. Sage likes her a lot."

Wade huffed. "Too bad she's related to the Kenos."

"Distantly," Yates said. "She hates this conflict and wants it ended. So do I."

"So do we all," Wade said, "but the ball is in the Kenos' court."

"No, it isn't. Let me tell you something. After the places I've been, the real conflicts I've seen, I think it's *all* senseless." His voice rose. "All of it. I don't want any more. For my part, this Keno trouble is over, especially where Laurel is concerned."

Wade pointed a pistol finger. "That's because you like her."

"And what's wrong with that?" Bowie asked.

Leave it to his cousin to seek balance and peace.

"We're friends trying to help three little kids. It's not a romance." Couldn't be, not with his spine full of doomsday shrapnel. No matter how much he cared about her.

Or maybe because he cared so much.

Wade looked toward the ceiling. "Thank goodness for that."

"I'm bringing her and the three Stafford children to the ranch Saturday afternoon to see the horses."

Wade leveled a squinting gaze. "Kind of rushing things, aren't you?"

No, he wasn't. He was already eight years late.

"There's one other thing I need to get off my chest."

"We're listening." Wade propped his elbows on the desk.

Pulse rattling like a marble in a pop can, Yates blurted the words. "I said this once and you ignored me, so I'll say it clearer this time. You had nothing to do with what happened to Trent. Nothing. If I ever let you think differently, I was wrong. *I* was the man in charge, not you. I don't blame you. Stop blaming yourself."

While his brother's mouth dropped open and a dozen emotions flickered over his face, Yates jerked upright and spun toward the doorway. The quick movements shot sparks down his back and leg. An involuntary hiss escaped him.

Though the effort took everything he could muster, he forced himself to march out of the room as if he wasn't in agony.

He'd had his say. He'd gotten two important things out in the open.

The rest was his to carry alone.

Laurel got the call from the home health nurse on Saturday morning. She was sitting at her kitchen bar, sipping sweet coffee and looking forward to the day ahead with Yates and the kids at the Sundown Ranch.

But trouble had a way of changing the best-laid plans.

An emergency situation had arisen, and the nurse didn't know who else to call.

Stephen Stafford was being admitted to the hospital. Someone needed to care for the Stafford children.

"Who's looking after them now?" Laurel asked.

"I am at the moment, but I have other patients to see and can't stay long. The children have nowhere to go. I know you care about them, so I was hoping you might be willing to help out until other arrangements can be made."

To Laurel's knowledge, the children had no extended family in the States. Their dad's only sister was a missionary teaching English somewhere in Southeast Asia.

The difficulties of juggling the troubled newspaper, taking the kids for hospital visits and to school, and caring for them every day filtered through Laurel's head. In the end, she couldn't refuse. The kids needed her. "Tell Stephen not to worry. I'll look after them."

"Thank you. He was reluctant to ask, although he has a fear about them going into foster care."

"That won't happen if I can help it. Give me ten minutes and I'll be there."

Laurel hung up, grabbed her keys and rushed to the car. On the drive, she phoned Yates to let him know she was headed to the hospital, not to his ranch.

His reaction was the same as hers.

"I'll be there as soon as I can."

"You don't have to. I've got it."

A beat passed and then, "The kids need us, Laurel. I'm coming."

She needed him too. "Thank you."

A short time later, as she twisted Chelsey's hair into a long braid, Yates strode into the Stafford house, Justice at his side. His gaze found hers and held on.

Her silly pulse bumped a couple of extra times.

He'd trimmed his dark beard again, this time to barely there. Beneath those piercing blue eyes, the scruff was appealing.

Decidedly so.

Since his return to Sundown Valley, he'd gained weight and didn't look quite so gaunt and pale. He'd been handsome before. Now he was a heart crusher.

She should know.

Still, everything in her strained toward him. Foolishness, but she could not stop the flow of feelings for the man who'd broken her heart.

"Are they doing okay?" Yates asked softly.

Laurel nodded. "Sadly, they've been through their dad's hospitalizations before."

"What about you?" he asked. "You look a little shell-shocked."

Lauren forced a laugh. "You could say that."

"Hey." He skimmed his fingertips over her shoulder. "We got this. Together. Whatever you need."

She loved the sound of that, although she knew what he meant. He was moral support. That was all.

But her heart didn't think so.

"Right. Good. Thank you for being here."

"No thanks needed, Laurel. I care about these kids too."

Yes, about the kids. That's the way it was supposed to be. If she still ached with the knowledge that she wasn't all that important to Yates, the problem was hers, not his. He'd never promised her anything.

Nodding, she patted Chelsey's braid and released her. "All done, sweetie. Go brush your teeth and pack your overnight bag."

"We're having a sleepover at Laurel's," Chelsey announced to Yates as she headed toward her room.

"Sounds like fun." Yates cocked an eyebrow toward Laurel. "Pillow fights?"

"Oh, spare me."

He grinned. The result was devastatingly handsome.

"I'm still trying to figure out sleeping arrangements for everyone."

"Sleeping bags," Yates said. "We have some at the ranch you can borrow. A tent too. They can pretend to camp out in your guest room." He stopped, eyebrows knit together. "You do have a guest room, don't you?"

"Yes, and your idea is brilliant. We'll make it fun, a camping trip to my house."

"I'll bring the s'mores."

She laughed. "I don't have a firepit."

"I'll bring that too." He winked. "Teamwork."

In five minutes flat, Yates had made her more confident about this sudden, unexpected turn of events. She could do this. With his help.

Aiden rushed in from the hallway and threw his arms around his hero's legs. "I knew you'd come!"

Yates, Laurel noted with some concern, grimaced as he took the force of the boy's body against his.

The minimum impact had caused him discomfort.

Megan, not to be outdone, rushed him too. Yates caught her shoulders before she could slam into him. "Let me see those braids of yours. You sure look pretty."

Megan caressed the end of a braid, careful not to dislodge the red bows. "Laurel did them. Can we go get pancakes? I'm hungry."

"What time are we going to see Daddy?" Aiden gazed up at the tall man, his face worried.

Yates crouched to his level. "We'll figure that out after breakfast. Okay?"

"I guess." Aiden was clearly old enough to be more worried about his dad than his younger sisters were.

Justice felt the boy's anxiety and nudged his small hand. Aiden went to his knees and buried his face in the dog's fur.

"I'm starved." Yates patted his belly to cement the lie.

He'd told her about his diminished appetite and how hard he had to work to gain weight. "How do pancakes sound to the rest of you?"

The girls sent up a cheer of "Pancakes, pancakes, pancakes."

Laurel laughed. "Ah, the resilience of childhood."

Yates winked. "The docs probably won't let us in to see the kids' dad for a while anyway. Might as well fill up our bellies."

"Are we still going to your ranch to see the horses?" Aiden asked.

Yates patted the boy's shoulder. "Let's check on your dad first and then decide, okay?"

"Daddy's gonna be all right," Chelsey said as she dragged a backpack into the living room. "He's always better after the doctors fix him."

Laurel swallowed a lump in her throat.

She hoped the little girl was right.

She wasn't.

Yates stepped into the hospital corridor with Laurel and a scrub-clad doctor he didn't know. The physician wanted to speak to them alone, without the children. Never a good sign.

"Mr. Stafford's condition continues to deteriorate. He needs care that neither home health nor this hospital can provide. I'm recommending a specialized long term–care facility."

Laurel gasped. "But the children…"

"Mr. Stafford and I have discussed this. He knows it's for the best. He can no longer care for himself or the kids, but, like you, he's also worried about what will happen to them. He mentioned a sister?" The doctor's voice rose on the question.

"She's out of the country."

"Do you know how to reach her?"

Laurel shook her head. "No."

Yates heard the tears in the back of Laurel's throat and hated that she was upset. He edged closer until their hands touched.

"We'll find a way." His stomach rolled from the short stack, bacon and eggs he'd forced down his throat as well from as his concern for the children.

"The only other option is temporary foster care." The doctor looped a stethoscope over his shoulders. "This hospital is obligated to notify child services unless other arrangements are made."

"I told Stephen I would take the children," Laurel said.

"Even though it may be weeks or months instead of days? That's a big responsibility."

Laurel gazed at the closed hospital door as if she could see the children through it huddled around their dad, waiting for him to come home. Only this time, he wouldn't. Not for a long time. Maybe not ever.

Yates saw the thoughts tumbling behind Laurel's eyes. She was a single woman with a struggling business in dire need of her attention. She already cared for a difficult old lady with health challenges. And she had no one to help her.

Except him.

He entwined his fingers with hers and squeezed. "Remember what I told you. We can do this. You're not in this alone."

Didn't he owe her that much? And more? This, at last, was a way to pay recompense.

And, if he was honest, to spend more time with the woman he'd never been able to forget.

Laurel turned her face to meet his eyes. After two heartbeats, she smiled.

"Yes. Whatever they need. We'll handle it."

Together, he wanted to say, they could handle anything. Except the truth.

Gran wasn't enthused.

"What on earth are you thinking, Laurel Elizabeth?"

"Shh. They'll hear you."

Gran made an impatient gesture. "The three of them are so exhausted they passed out the minute they climbed into those sleeping bags. They won't hear anything until tomorrow. What did you and that Trudeau boy do to them, anyway?"

The morning may have started out with a hospitalization, but the afternoon had been perfect. Laurel didn't say that, of course. Gran would have an even bigger fit if she knew how much Laurel enjoyed the time with Yates.

"We led them around on horses, took them fishing, let them run and play. Nothing special."

"Well, you wore them out, that's for sure." Gran smacked her lips—whether in approval or aggravation, Laurel wasn't sure. Probably the latter.

"I suppose," Gran went on, "that's a good thing, considering the circumstances. Do they have any idea what's happening? Have you told them their dad is about to be shipped off to Dallas while they remain here until somebody in some foreign outpost can be contacted and decides if she wants them?"

Gran hadn't had the breath to string that many words together in a long time. Getting fired up must be good for her pulmonary function.

"Yes, we told them today."

"'We'? By 'we,' I take it to mean you and that Trudeau boy." She made a disgusted sound.

"Yes. His name is Yates, by the way. He's offered to help me with the kids."

Gran's lips tightened like a drawstring. "What help

would a Trudeau be? I'm telling you, girl, you're asking for trouble with that man. He'll bring nothing but grief upon your head."

He couldn't cause her any more grief than before. This time she was armed with the knowledge that falling in love could hurt. So she wouldn't. Even though love was beautiful, exhilarating, fulfilling. Until it wasn't.

Yes, she loved his company. She loved his laugh and his voice and intelligence. She was even intrigued by the air of mystery that surrounded him.

But none of those things equated to romantic love.

"If there is trouble, Gran, it's mine, not yours. Yates is concerned for the children. So am I. As you should be."

Gran ruffled up like an angry hen. "Well, of course I am. I raised you, didn't I? I can certainly show kindness to those poor little children. Even if they are noisy and messy."

Laurel leaned in and kissed her grandmother's cheek. "Thank you, Gran. I love you."

"Oh, go on with you," the older woman blustered. "But mark my words about that Trudeau boy. He's up to no good."

Sunday afternoon, Yates parked outside Laurel's house. He'd never been inside. Foolish on his part. Eight years ago—nearly nine, now—he should have knocked on that door, introduced himself to her dad and grandma, and asked her out. No secrets. No family tangles. Just him and Laurel.

Now it was too late for anything except a friendship.

He didn't like to think of himself as a coward, but he had been.

Back then, he'd found the secret game exciting. Today, as a man with plenty of world experience, he saw how immature he had been. He'd been old enough to run a ranch and take over the care of his brothers and Bowie after their parents died, but he'd been sorely lacking in maturity.

"Ready to run the gauntlet, Justice?" he asked as he unbuckled their respective seat belts.

Justice hopped to the ground and trotted up the concrete steps as if he knew exactly who was inside.

Maybe he did.

Yates's pulse tripped a couple of times as he followed. He moved carefully so his feet wouldn't stumble too.

His hip had been cranky all day. Probably slept crooked. Tomorrow was physical therapy and a meeting with his doctors at the VA.

He wanted to pray for encouraging news, but what good would that do? He knew what was permanently lodged against his spine.

God had made it clear—He wasn't into performing back surgery.

Laurel opened the front door just as he leaned hard on the porch pillar for leverage up the steps.

Her journalist's eyes watched him as if she suspected his infirmity.

He turned loose of the post and forced his legs to carry him to the door.

Laurel stood to one side and let him in. "I didn't know you were coming by."

He stood in the entryway, looking around. The inside of the house smelled like her. And bacon. He appreciated both scents.

"Does Grandma own a gun?"

She laughed and rolled her eyes. "She knows you're going to be around to help with the kids."

"That doesn't answer my question." He allowed a wry grin.

"Don't worry, brave soldier boy, I'll protect you."

"You and my dog."

"Hello, Justice." She patted the animal and then to Yates said, "Want some sweet tea?"

"Thanks. Sounds good. Where are the kids?" He followed her from the small living space through a doorway to an equally small, old-fashioned eat-in kitchen.

"Out in the back with Gran, learning the finer points of which plants they better not trample and which flowers are okay to pick." She took two shiny glasses down from a shelf.

"Drill sergeant."

"She'd have made a good one. I think she's the reason my dad was so driven to make the paper succeed. Gran pushes hard for what she thinks is important."

She filled the glasses with ice and tea and handed him one.

"The kids doing okay today?"

"So far. They're a little clingy at times, and I can tell they're anxious. Especially Aiden. He's old enough to realize his life is changing, and yet he doesn't know what to expect. I don't want to tell him either. Everything is up in the air."

She motioned toward the round wooden table for four. There were five in this house now. An extra chair had been crowded into one corner.

The two of them sat, tea glasses between them.

"A social worker is trying to reach Stephen's sister, Katherine, in Thailand. He's not exactly sure where she is but has a contact number through the agency she works for." Laurel rubbed her fingers down the condensing glass. "I think he'll feel better after they talk. I know Aiden will."

"What about you? How are *you* handling all this?" he asked.

"Me? I'm fine. You know I adore these kids. And I pray a lot. Lots and lots of prayer."

"I wished that made a difference."

"Of course it does." She looked at him in surprise. "God hears the prayer of every Christian. He loves us and wants what's best for all of us."

"Does He? Doesn't seem that way to me. If He really cared, Stephen wouldn't be too sick to care for his own kids. His wife wouldn't have died. They wouldn't be living with a stranger, hoping that some aunt they barely know will take them in."

My parents and brother would be alive. And I wouldn't be plagued with the worry of paralysis. Or the guilt of what I'd done to my baby brother.

Laurel leaned back against her chair and stared at him for a long, silent moment. "You have a lot built up inside you, Yates. Want to tell me what's going on with you?"

He gave a short, mirthless laugh. "Not particularly."

The retro-green clock on the wall above the table clicked to the next number. Laurel remained silent, as if waiting for him to say something.

Words fomented inside him, things he'd carried since the day Trent died and he'd been too guilt-ridden to properly grieve.

Yates stared around the room, breathing hard as if he'd run up a tall, rugged hill.

He didn't expect Laurel to understand what he barely understood himself. She hadn't lost half her family to tragedy.

"All the prayer in the world won't stop disasters from happening. Or change the past. If God pays any attention to us at all, He's only watching the action, not doing anything about it."

"I don't believe that in the least. Neither did you at one time."

He waved away the reminder of his once rock-solid faith. "Long time ago. When I was a kid. Before too many people I loved died. Now I know better."

"You're wrestling with your anger, Yates, not with your faith. You know God is real. You know He'll never leave nor forsake you. And you know you need Him in your life. You're just too proud and stubborn to let go of your anger so He can heal you. You need someone to blame for your losses, so it's Him."

"Some things even He can't heal." Or won't.

"It's true. He doesn't always heal or answer prayer the way we hope, but He can."

"If He wants to."

"If I didn't believe God has our best interest at heart, I'm not sure I could tolerate this life." She put her hand on top of his. Her skin was cool and damp from the glass. "Yates, I don't understand all you've been through. You hide so much of yourself from the rest of the world. But I know you well enough to see that you're struggling. I recognize a man who needs God and is too angry to admit it."

He slid his hand from beneath hers and glanced away. Looking into her clear, earnest eyes muddled his thoughts. "Do we have to talk about this?"

"Being mad at God isn't helping you."

She was right about that. He'd wrestled with his thoughts half the night and again this morning when Wade had pressed him to attend church. He felt bottled up, carbonated. If he released all that bubbled inside him, he'd spew his anger and hurt and confusion on everyone he loved.

He couldn't do that. Wouldn't. Not if he loved them.

The word ambled across his brain and lingered there. *Love.*

Looking back at Laurel, he saw in her eyes the tenderness, kindness, goodness that was her essence. He also saw something else. Something he'd vowed not to allow. Even if he was afraid he felt it too.

Another impossibility that God had put in his path. More heartache to deal with.

He looked down at the amber liquid in his glass. The color of her eyes.

No matter where he looked, Laurel was there.

"I care about you, Yates."

"I know." He longed to say the words back to her, but he forced them to remain inside.

"Promise me you'll try to find your way back to the Savior. At least pray about whatever is eating you alive. Ask Him for help. What have you got to lose?"

A recon scout worked alone. He didn't need help. He needed no one. Not God. Not her.

She touched his hand again.

And Yates knew he was lying.

Chapter Ten

An air of despair hung over the entire newspaper office. Even the usually chipper, sweet-roll-toting Tansy looked glum at her desk in the cluttered cubicle where she worked.

Heart heavy, Laurel stared through the plate glass dividing her office from the rest of the newsroom. Her dad's name, still emblazoned on the window, mocked her.

George Maxwell, Publisher-Editor.

"Dad wouldn't have let this happen. He'd have thought of something to stop the flow of red ink over our ledgers," she muttered.

The whole morning had been like this. First, Chelsey had cried for ten minutes over a purple sock she couldn't find. Aiden had argued against going to school. And Megan had wanted her daddy.

On top of that fiasco, Gran had roamed the house, dragging her oxygen gear and mumbling about someone being in over her head.

In other words, Laurel was failing miserably on both the home front and at work.

Her cell phone chirped. She glanced at the fancy, high-tech device. Yates.

After their talk the other day, she'd prayed about him and for him every day. He was suffering and, for reasons she didn't want to examine, his pain hurt her too.

If only he'd talk about whatever festered behind those blue eyes. Talk to her, but more importantly, talk to the

Lord, the only one who could do anything about whatever haunted him.

She didn't begin to understand the way God worked. She simply knew from experience that, after she prayed and put things in His hands, she felt better.

Laurel popped the heel of one hand against her forehead. "Father, forgive me. I'm badgering Yates to pray about his circumstances but failing to pray about my own."

Ignoring Yates's text, she pushed her computer and phone aside, closed her eyes, and prayed. For Yates, for the kids, for the newspaper.

She didn't know how long she prayed, but it was long enough that the weight began to lift from her chest.

Yates's ideas for the paper filtered through her thoughts. She'd barely considered them before. Had shoved them away like old news, afraid to change, afraid to take a chance of making things worse. Afraid of her dad's and Gran's disapproval.

What if Yates was right? Maybe the *Times* needed to change with the times.

Smiling at her clever turn of phrase, she went to the door of her office and yelled, "Tansy, come in here."

Tansy's chair clattered as she rolled away from her cubicle to frown at Laurel. "What's up?"

"I have an idea to run past you."

"Good. I'm all out." She held up one finger. "One minute. From the look on your face, I'll need coffee and carbs for this."

Laurel shook her head, cheered. Interesting how much more hopeful she felt after talking to Jesus. Yates was wrong: prayer definitely helped.

Tansy entered the office, plunked refreshments on Laurel's desk and tugged the straight-backed chair closer. "Is this about that man whose name I shall not speak because you get mad if I say anything negative? Or is it about the newspaper or about the Stafford kids or your sick grandma? Girl, you have too much going on in your world."

"The paper. We're at work. I'll figure out the rest of my life later. And his name is Yates. I like him. He's kind to the kids. His dog likes me. And he is not the cause of my problems."

Tansy rolled her eyes. "He's also handsome, well-heeled and off-limits."

"He is not off-limits. We aren't doing the off-limits thing anymore. Remember?"

Tansy made a humming sound. "But he *is* the other two. Dreamy handsome, money in his pockets, broody mysterious."

"That's three."

"And you have a thing for him. A really major thing."

Laurel waved off the conversation, which never got anywhere productive. Tansy tried, but she couldn't trust Yates. That Laurel *did* boggled Tansy's orderly mind.

"Newspaper business, Tansy. Concentrate."

"Concentrating." The slender woman chomped into an apricot Danish. Today's T-shirt stated, *I'm silently correcting your grammar.*

"Yates had an idea."

"There he is again."

"Hush. I want to know your thoughts on his idea."

"I hate it." Tansy grinned to show she was joking.

"What if we changed our newspaper's focus away from national and world news?"

"Seriously? But that's what we're known for. We've won awards."

Dad had won awards. "Except those things aren't selling newspapers. When we ran that article on Yates—"

Tansy pointed her sweet roll. "I thought this conversation was not about Yates."

Laurel ignored her. "His article garnered more sales than we've seen in a long time."

"Then we immediately went bust again."

"Exactly. Don't you see? Maybe we'd sell more papers if we run more articles on local things, local business, local people—maybe even some chatty, folksy pieces about clubs and churches and school activities."

Tansy stared at her, chewing thoughtfully.

Laurel waited. Tansy would wallow and figure before she expressed an opinion. Her ability to analyze a situation was one of the reasons Laurel trusted her.

"Consider this." Tansy put her Danish on a napkin and wiped her hands down the sides of her black leggings, leaving behind speckles of white icing. "Let's try this concept on one or two pages for a week or two. Add an online survey for feedback of what kind of news readers find most interesting."

"I like it. We still maintain the integrity of Dad's hard news while trying something new."

"What if it works? What if people love it? Are you willing to completely change the direction of the *Times*?"

Laurel blew out a long sigh between her lips. She sounded like a horse. Which reminded her of Yates. "I don't know. Change is scary. Gran will hate it."

"Here. Take a Danish and think about it more. Meanwhile—" she stood up and dusted the white frosting from her pants to the wooden floor "—I'm off to find some human interest stories. I rock at that, you know. People like to tell me things, and they *love* to gossip."

"Isn't gossip a sin?"

"Not the kind that sells newspapers."

Yates took the long way home.

He'd spent all morning and half the afternoon shuffling between surgeons, neurologists, physical therapists and the VA hospital's X-ray department. His body ached from the therapy. His head hurt from hoping things would have changed for the better.

They hadn't.

"Stable," he muttered to the cab of his truck, wishing he hadn't left Justice at home. The dog was a good listener. And he didn't spread tales.

Yates didn't much like the word *stable*. He wanted to be well and free from the pieces of metal impinging the nerves in his spine.

Better stable than the alternative, though.

Same instructions as before. Keep up the exercise regimen. Eat well. No heavy lifting. No sudden twists or jerks. He hadn't even asked about getting on a horse. One buck off could turn him into a yard dart and be the end of his mobility.

At present he could still walk on his own.

It was the what-ifs that gnawed at him.

He mulled and fretted for many miles, but by the time he reached the city limits sign welcoming him to Sundown Valley, he'd pep-talked himself into some semblance of cheer for the Stafford kids' sake.

Using his Bluetooth, he phoned Laurel. Hearing her voice always uplifted his mood, even if she nagged about his relationship, or lack thereof, with God.

She nagged because she cared. He was smart enough to understand that, and the knowledge created a tangled knot in his chest.

What kind of woman forgave so easily? Was it due to her strong faith?

He certainly didn't deserve her…friendship. Or whatever it was.

"Hey," he said when he heard her voice on the other end of the signal. Fact was, hearing her silky voice shot a pleasant tingle down his spine. Pleasant. Not painful.

She was good medicine.

"How'd the appointments go?"

"Fine." Before she could ask for details, he hurried on. "Gained a few pounds, added some muscle. Except for PT, docs cut me loose for six months."

"That's great news, Yates. I'm glad you're healing."

He wasn't. He was *stable*.

"I'm back in town. Want me to pick up the kids from school?"

"Would you mind? I'm pretty busy here."

"No problem. Glad to do it." He didn't want her to hang up, so he asked, "What's got you so busy at the paper?"

"You."

"Me?" He liked the sound of that.

"Your ideas. We're scrapping the last two pages of business and financial news to add more local human interest articles. Temporarily."

"Worth a try."

"That's what Tansy said."

"Did she know it was my idea?"

"She did. She's coming around, Yates. So is Gran."

He chuckled wryly. "Must be my dog. He wins hearts."

She shocked him by saying, "So do you."

He let a beat pass while he contemplated her meaning. Finally, he relegated it to the "making friendly conversation" pile.

They were good friends, teammates. Well, except for those goodnight kisses that seemed to grow in intensity as time passed.

"I'll take the kids to see their dad at the hospital, if you'd like, and then to the park. Save you the trip. Call me when you leave work, and I'll bring them to your house."

"Scared of being alone with Gran?"

He chuckled. "Just hankering for more time at a hospital."

Laurel laughed, but her tone was sympathetic. "You don't have to take them to see Stephen. I can do that later tonight."

"Later tonight I want to watch a movie with you, not hang out in a hospital." He'd done enough of that to last him two lifetimes.

"Stephen's being transferred to Dallas on Wednesday. The arrangements have been made."

Tough deal. Yates knew a lot about rehab centers. He'd talk to Stephen tonight about what to expect. "Did he ever reach his sister?"

"Someone did. She's coming for the children as soon as she can work out the logistics. The best part is, she plans to settle in Dallas, near Stephen's rehab facility."

Yates got a funny feeling about letting the trio go. He could only imagine how much harder it would be for Laurel. "That's good, I guess. The kids can maintain contact during Stephen's recovery."

If the guy recovered.

"Stephen's relieved. He says his sister loves kids, especially his. She always wanted children but never found the right guy to marry, so she teaches. They'll do well with her and with their dad nearby."

He heard the throb in her voice. She was another woman who'd always wanted children. "You'll miss them."

"I will. Now that we've more or less adjusted to being together, the house will seem empty without them."

"Yeah." She deserved to marry the best man on earth and fill her home with all the kids she wanted.

Thinking about her with another man made his stomach churn.

He feared he was falling in love with her, but letting her know was out of the question. He refused to be a burden to anyone, especially her.

Loving meant sacrifice. Hadn't he learned that in the

military? A man loved his country and freedom and was willing to sacrifice to keep them.

Except he couldn't keep Laurel, not in the way he wanted to. He'd be sacrificing *not* to keep her.

The long elementary building came into sight.

"I'm nearly at the school. Talk to you later. All the best with the news articles. I hope they sell a ton of papers."

"Me too. Thanks."

They hung up and he parked outside Sundown Valley Elementary. A little early, he sorted through his phone contacts and began sending out texts urging his friends and relatives to buy subscriptions to the *Times*.

Big changes are coming. Don't miss out, he typed, grinning a little at his sudden marketing inspiration.

He couldn't marry Laurel and give her kids, but he could sell newspapers for her.

Glancing at his watch, he saw that the time for picking up Megan was nearing. Five more minutes. Her pre-K class released first and required an authorized adult to be physically present before she could leave her teacher's care. No running out to the waiting car.

He liked that. Safety. The world could be a mean place. And Megan was an innocent rose.

Stepping out of the truck and onto the paved parking lot, he was shocked to find Bud Keno blocking his path.

"What are you doing here?" he asked.

"Picking up my grandson. Saw you pull up and thought I'd remind you of our little chat at the ball game."

"I'm too busy for this."

"That's what I hear. You and Laurel are busy playing house with someone else's kids."

"None of your business." Yates started to move around the other man.

Keno shoved him. Balance always precarious, Yates stumbled back against the truck. His off-kilter body slammed against the metal. He heard the fiberglass door pop, felt the sudden jarring of his bones. Pain pinged up his spine and down his left leg.

He sucked in an unbidden hiss.

"I'm talking to you, boy," Keno said through clenched teeth. "Don't act like you're better than me." He poked a finger into Yates's chest. "All you Trudeaus think you're special, think you run this county and everyone in it. I got news for you—you don't. I know who you are and what you did."

Trying to get his pain under control was one thing. Keeping his temper in check was another.

An inner battle raged. Plow his fist into the guy's face and get it over with or walk away. His chest rose and fell, breathing accelerated, either from the pain or the anger. Maybe both.

The school bell rang. Car doors slammed. Buses pulled into the circle in front of the school building.

He clenched and unclenched his fists, fought for control.

A scout with self-control lived to fight again another day.

He drew in a long breath and let it ease out as he raised both hands in mock surrender.

The calm in his voice was what he'd aimed for, but it still surprised him. "We're on school grounds. Settle down and go get your grandson."

"I don't take orders from you."

Yates sighed. He couldn't win with this guy.

The chatter and calls of children penetrated the tense atmosphere. Bud turned his attention toward them and then back to Yates.

A mean little smile tilted the corners of Bud's mouth.

"I'm thinking of taking off a whole afternoon to make phone calls. To Laurel and her grandma. Another to your brother. Should be fun."

"Leave them out of this, Bud. I'm warning you."

"Or what? I'm in the driver's seat here, boy, and I think your family needs to know where you were the day your brother died."

Yates's blood ran cold. This was the secret Bud knew. Not just that Yates and Laurel had secretly dated but that they'd been together when he was supposed to be on the ranch, watching over his brothers.

A mean-spirited man like Bud Keno would love using that information to hurt those he considered enemies.

"They say revenge is best served cold," Bud went on. "I've been biding my time to get back at Wade since he called the sheriff on me."

"I don't know anything about that."

"Doesn't matter. Wade knows. And won't I have fun telling him that you were playing footsie with a Keno while a wild bull killed your little brother?" Bud smacked his fat lips as if tasting something sweet. "The thought of shoving that bit of news in Wade's arrogant face and stirring bad blood between the two of you thrills my soul. Maybe I'll even put an announcement in Laurel's paper."

Yates's gut squeezed. He thought he might be sick. The weight of his own culpability nearly brought him to his knees.

"What do you want, Keno?"

"Well, let's see. I've waited eight years for this, though the timing couldn't be better. I should be rewarded for my restraint." Bud eased back a little and stroked his chin as if he didn't already have some diabolical plan in mind. "Two things. Stop seeing Laurel."

For Laurel's sake, to keep her from finding out and feeling responsible, he could stop seeing her. He wouldn't want to, but he could. "And the other?"

"That's a mighty fine stallion you've got at your place.

He sure throws some beautiful colts. I imagine they bring a pretty penny too."

Blood pumping hard enough to explode his chest, Yates faked a calm he didn't feel.

"What are you getting at, Keno?"

"I've kinda taken a hankering for him. Sign over your stallion to me, and I'll forget what I know."

Excalibur? Keno wanted Excalibur in exchange for silence?

The stallion was Yates's most prized possession. Somehow Keno knew that.

"What you suggest is extortion, blackmail."

"Ain't it, though?" Bud's ruddy cheeks creased. "I doubt you'll call the law."

Yates's thoughts raced, sorting and contemplating.

Another bell rang from the school building.

He was a problem solver. He needed time to think.

Defuse the bomb. Save the day. Get some distance and figure this thing out.

Even if retreat was humiliating to a soldier.

The other man had the upper hand and he knew it.

"I'll think about it."

Yates was protecting his family and Laurel, not himself. That made all the difference. For them, he could take Keno's abuse and threats. For them, he could give up the stallion if he had to and carry this guilt to his grave. For Laurel, he could walk away. Again.

"Think long and hard, boy. Long and hard. I don't bluff."

Keno glared at him for a couple more seconds, then snickered and ambled with cocky confidence toward the school.

Chapter Eleven

"**Y**ou're awfully quiet tonight," Laurel said. "Is something wrong?"

She'd noticed the minute Yates arrived at her home with the children. She'd have thought his mood was the result of an unsatisfactory visit with his doctors or with Stephen Stafford but had decided that was not his problem. The children were full of chatter about their day, their dad, the playtime at the park when they'd fed peanuts to a squirrel that sat on his haunches and begged.

Yates said little.

"Lot on my mind," he replied after she stared at him for a long, silent moment.

"I see that." She offered him another slice of pizza. He'd bought the extra-large and a bowl of salad, but he wasn't eating much.

The kids, on the other hand, were devouring the pizza and ignoring the salad. Their dad, apparently, stuck to healthier choices, and pizza was a rare treat.

Yates took a slice from the offered box, catching the string of cheese on one finger. Unlike the children, he didn't play with it, nor did he eat it. He dropped it on his plate.

"You said the doctors' appointments went well." Hadn't he said that?

"As expected. No big news on that front. I talked to Stephen about his transfer too." His blue eyes slid toward the trio seated around the table. "The kids know. Stephen made the Dallas move sound exciting."

"Well," she said in a falsely chipper voice, aware three small sets of ears listened. "Dallas is an exciting city. They'll love making new friends there."

"But I'll miss my old friends," Aiden piped up, settling his focus on Yates.

Yates's throat convulsed. "I'll miss you, too, buddy. All your pals will miss you—but hey, you can always video chat with us the way you did with your aunt."

"Yeah, I guess." The boy heaved a sigh. "I like being with you, though. You know, in real life instead of inside the computer."

Yates winked. "I like hanging out with you too. And once you get settled, I may even drive down to Dallas to see you."

"Cool! Did you hear that, Chelsey? Yates will come and visit, even after we move away."

Chelsey's dark eyes lit up. "Will you come, too, Laurel?"

Laurel exchanged glances with the man making the promises. Her heart fluttered as she considered all those hours on the road with Yates. Perhaps it wasn't wise, but she admitted to herself, she'd enjoy every moment.

"Plenty of room in my truck." He winked again, this time at her. "If her grandma will let her hang out with Bigfoot."

Laurel swallowed a laugh. Annoyed that anyone with Keno DNA entertained a Trudeau under her roof, Gran disappeared into her room every time Yates showed up. Muttering all the way down the hall, she slammed the bedroom door for good measure.

Tonight she'd been so aggravated to discover him eating pizza in her kitchen that she'd turned her television up loud enough to drown out any hint of his voice.

Laurel refused to argue about it anymore. She'd made

her decision not to perpetuate the feud and said so. Furious, Gran called her a traitor, warning that nothing good could ever come from Laurel's friendship with a Trudeau. Especially one as damaged and moody as Yates.

Gran claimed that if Laurel was too blind to see the danger signs, she'd pay a steep price.

Megan, who was currently picking the pepperoni off her pizza and feeding it to a delighted Justice, seemed oblivious to the current discussion about Gran or the move to Dallas.

Like most four-year-olds, she tended toward self-focus. Aiming soft brown eyes at Yates, she asked, "Who was the man you were talking to at my school today? He looked mean."

Yates's expression went flat. Gazing down at his plate, he slowly put the half-eaten pizza down.

When he spoke, his voice sounded tense. "No one for you to worry about, Megan."

Laurel frowned. He should know such an evasive answer aroused her journalist curiosity. His reaction was odd at best.

"Yates? Is that what has you in such a solemn mood? Who was that man?"

He met her eyes and then swept a panoramic glance around the three children. "No one for you to worry about either."

She didn't like that answer. And he wouldn't get away with it. But apparently, he didn't want to discuss the man in front of the children.

Which made her only that much more curious.

Yates had planned to make his getaway after dinner, but Megan, with the soft brown eyes he couldn't resist, had pleaded with him to stay long enough to read a bedtime story. She liked his funny voices.

"She's especially clingy tonight," Laurel whispered as

the little girl dragged her stuffed rabbit toward the guest bedroom she and her sister shared.

What could he do? He stayed. Spending more time with Laurel wasn't exactly a chore.

With Keno's ultimatum hanging over his head, every moment with her seemed even more precious.

Though he'd never entered her house in the old days, he'd driven past it more times than he could count. Wanting to see her. Wishing he had the temerity to knock on the door.

Sometimes he laughed at how immature he'd been back then. But there was nothing funny about his past behavior. Nothing at all.

The Maxwell home's interior wasn't big or fancy, but it exuded a coziness that surprised him. He hadn't expected warmth from Laurel's grandmother, who glared at him with enough coldness to freeze her eyelashes.

Laurel, on the other hand, was as warm as a June morning. Perhaps the cozy house was her doing. The children especially needed her warmth. Maybe he did too.

"Even though they're excited about the move, they're unsettled," he said. "Moving to a new city to live with an aunt is a big deal for little people."

He handed her the leftover parmesan packets. She stashed them in a nearby cabinet.

"Miss Laurel, I forgot to show you my note." Aiden, face shiny from his shower, appeared in the doorway of the kitchen, extending a slip of paper to Laurel. "It's okay if you don't want to."

She read the note from Aiden's teacher. "Cookies for a bake sale tomorrow? How long have you known about this?"

He shrugged. "I forgot."

Yates watched the struggle on the boy's face. He wanted to take those homemade cookies to school like all the other kids. But he wasn't comfortable enough in his new situation to say so.

Yates's chest pinched.

"Cookies?" Yates said. "Did you know I happen to be an expert cookie baker?"

Hope lit up the boy's face. "Really?"

"Absolutely." He patted his concave belly. "How do you think I got so fat?"

Aiden snickered. "You're skinny."

"I won't be after I bake those cookies. That is, if Laurel wants to help me." He hiked an eyebrow in her direction.

"I've never baked cookies with an expert before." Her eyes twinkled at Yates.

He liked that a lot. If he'd known baking cookies would please her, he'd have baked ten dozen on his first day back in town.

Making amends. Stealing every moment he could with her. Like before, but better, except for the danger of Bud Keno breathing down his neck.

He still didn't know what to do about the man's ultimatum.

Aiden's head ping-ponged from one adult to the other. Yates could read his thoughts: Was he getting cookies for school or not?

"You'll have your cookies, Aiden, when you wake up in the morning."

"Promise?"

"Yes. Now, get ready for bed. We have a date with a bedtime story first."

Aiden's small shoulders drooped dramatically. He groaned. "Not *Cinderella* again, please."

Yates laughed. The girls loved the story, but reading it for three nights in a row was trying Aiden's patience. "Deal."

After the story was read and the kids snuggled into their sleeping bags for the night, Yates turned his attention to the impromptu cookie baking with Laurel.

He couldn't say he was sorry about the last-minute note.

He shouldn't be this thrilled to spend more time with the woman he couldn't have. But he was.

Later, when he was home alone, he'd figure out what to do about Keno's conditions. He didn't trust Bud as far as he could jump, which wasn't far. Even if Yates did his bidding, there was no guarantee Bud would keep his word. The man enjoyed hurting others, especially a Trudeau. Laurel was simply collateral in the path of his vendetta.

"Yates?" Laurel's voice broke into his troubled thoughts.

Shaking his head, he clapped his hands and said with forced cheer, "Where do we start?"

"You're the expert," she said, which made him smile as he trailed her from the kids' room into the small old-fashioned kitchen.

Laurel was good at distracting him.

"We need sugar," he said. "Lots of sugar."

With a wry twist of her lips, she asked, "Is that it, Chef Cookie Expert?"

He whipped out his phone and thumbed through until he found a list of cookies. "What kind do you like?"

Laurel tilted sideways to glance at his phone and then opened several cabinet doors, peering inside each one.

"I don't bake very often," she said. "Gran can't handle the sugar, and I get more than enough from Tansy's constant supply of sweets from the bakery. Looks like I have ingredients for oatmeal or sugar cookies. Which kind do you think he'll want?"

"You pick. I like both."

Laurel gave him a look. "You're no help."

"Sad but true."

She shoved a box of oats against his chest. "You know I'm joking." Opening a drawer, she pulled out a white apron. "Turn around."

He stared at the strip of girly cloth as if it was a grenade. "I don't need that."

"Humor me."

Eyes rolled so high he went temporarily blind, Yates turned his back to her. She slid her arms around his waist to put the apron in place.

With Laurel's warmth against his back, Yates couldn't help himself. At least, that's the argument he used.

When she snugged the strings tight, he turned, tugged her into his arms and stood smiling down at her.

Head tilted back to look up at him, she smiled in return. "I like when you do that."

"What? Wear an apron?"

Her lips pursed. He thought about kissing them.

"Hold me," she said. "Smile at me. As if you're happy to be with me."

Dangerous ground.

"I am," he admitted. Then, because she made him happy in ways he'd forgotten about, he kissed her forehead. Then her nose. And her chin.

She laughed, grabbed his scruffy chin and smooched him on the lips. Quick and friendly and completely unsatisfactory. He'd had something *more* in mind.

Laurel stepped back. "We better get busy on these cookies. I have work tomorrow."

Though kissing was infinitely more fun, it was also more dangerous.

Yates turned his focus to the baking. He hadn't been joking about his cooking skills. He knew his way around a kitchen.

"Oatmeal," he said as she indicated the mixing bowls on a shelf over her head. "My specialty. Got any raisins?"

He easily reached the biggest bowl. The shelves were neatly arranged, small bowls nesting in bigger ones, lids aligned in some kind of lid rack. Tidy, like her.

While he looked around for a spoon, Laurel opened drawers and cabinets, took out the needed utensils and ingredients. "Yes. I bought those little boxes for the kids' lunches. They love them."

"That works."

They bumped and jostled in the small space, flirting a little more than was prudent.

He always enjoyed his time with her, but tonight felt different. Domestic.

He—a man who'd spent most of his life in the pastures and woods and, for the last eight years, in nearly uninhabitable places—was not a domestic animal.

Yet he felt like one with this woman at his side, kids asleep in the other room and an apron around his waist while he helped her bake cookies for a school bake sale. Even the military dog dozing in the corner looked domestic tonight.

He was having such a fine time that he barely noticed when she turned the conversation away from cookies.

"When we were eating pizza earlier," she said, dumping brown sugar into the bowl of butter while he stirred, "Megan asked you about a man you saw at the school. What was that about? Who was he and why did you react so oddly?"

The spoon paused in Yates's hands.

Even a recon scout, a trained watcher, a detail man like him—hadn't seen that coming.

"Not important."

"Then you shouldn't mind telling me." She cracked an egg and opened it over the bowl.

"You're persistent." He beat the soft dough with all his might, hoping to stem the flow of questions.

Laurel put a hand on the spoon handle. "Yes, I am. The more you resist, the more curious I become. So stop avoiding the question. Did it have something to do with the children?"

He sighed and shifted his weight to his good leg. "No."

"The army?"

He steered her away from that topic as quickly as possible. "No."

Nudging her hand aside, he returned to his task. The room grew quiet. Laurel measured out two cups of oats. He stirred them in, contemplating.

What would it hurt if he told her about some of Bud Keno's threats? She would know, but Wade and Bowie would remain in the dark about Yates's whereabouts on the day of Trent's death. Telling her would defuse Bud Keno's threats, at least those against her.

She wouldn't blame herself for that day, would she?

"I don't want you to feel responsible," he said, before he could think better of it.

"Now you *must* tell me what's going on. Obviously, this conversation concerns me."

"It does." He sighed again, considered tasting the cookie dough and then thought better of it since the cookies were for other people.

She placed a baking sheet on the counter next to the bowl. The metal clattered against the butcher block. Taking a can of pan spray from the pantry, she oiled the sheet.

The preheated oven beeped.

"This cookie dough smells good," he said.

"Cinnamon spice and vanilla. Yummy." She took out two teaspoons and handed him one. "I've heard you shouldn't eat raw cookie dough."

"Me too. Must be an old wives tale." He knew better.

"I don't think so. Something about the raw eggs."

"Live dangerously. Life's short."

"You should know about living dangerously."

He did. Boy, did he ever.

They dipped into the dough at the same time and laughed when their spoons clanked together.

Laurel pointed a loaded spoon at him. "In case this kills us, you should tell me everything you know."

Not everything. No way. Not the shrapnel. That was his own cross to bear. "Bud Keno."

With the tip of the spoon against her lips, she said, "That wasn't so difficult, was it? What did he want? To bury the hatchet?"

"In the top of my head."

She laughed and tasted the dough. "Good stuff. You *are* an expert."

"And you've yet to taste the finished product."

"I'm guessing Bud saw us together and wanted to cause trouble."

"He did. Like the sweet guy I am—" Yates pressed a hand against his heart, his tone wry "—I tried to explain that I wanted to be his best friend and roast s'mores around a campfire while singing Kumbaya or whatever best buddies do, but he wouldn't play fair. Threatened to tell my brother some things I'd rather keep to myself."

"Ah, more mysteries. Tell me."

She had a tiny speck of cookie dough on her bottom lip. He leaned in and kissed it away, hoping to distract her while he decided how much to say.

He still wrestled with Keno's demands, which he would not share with a soul. Excalibur was his to sell, keep or give away.

Laurel didn't allow his kiss to distract her. A disappointment for sure. She dipped to one side to begin plunking tablespoons of cookie dough onto the baking sheets.

Yates let a taste of sweet, buttery cookie dough melt on his tongue. Finally, he said, "It's about the day of Trent's accident."

Holding a wooden spoon aloft, she met his eyes. "Okay. This sounds serious."

"It is. Wade thought I blamed him for Trent's accident. I don't. I hope I've gotten that through his thick skull. The fault was mine."

"An accident is unintentional. Your brother's tragedy was no one's fault."

He wished he believed that. "Accidents can be avoided. Trent wouldn't have died if I'd been there."

"What makes you think that?"

"Because I never allowed Trent to go to the bull pen alone. We always went in pairs. We were extra careful with new bulls. They can be unpredictable and dangerous."

"What happened?"

"Trent went alone. I should have been with him. As the eldest, the head of the family, running the ranch and keeping everyone safe was my responsibility."

His stomach churned as he recalled that horrible moment when he'd seen his brother lying mangled and inert in the bull pen. The sweet cookie dough turned bitter on his tongue.

Laurel stopped adding dough to the baking sheet and slowly lay the spoon aside. "He was fourteen. You were barely in your twenties, a very young man bearing an enormous responsibility."

"It was mine to bear. Trent went to the bull pen alone because I had other plans that day." He swallowed. "You."

"Me?"

He raised his eyes to hers. "I was with you while my brother was dying. You were my excuse for not going with him. I wanted to be with you."

All the blood drained from Laurel's head. Dark speckles danced before her eyes.

"You must hate me."

"No." His tone was vehement. "Don't even go there. The fault was never yours. It was mine. All mine. I knew. You didn't."

"That's why you left? Why you joined the army so quickly?"

"I had to get away from here, from the memory, the

guilt." He huffed a short, mirthless laugh. "Guilt is like a shadow. It never leaves for long. When I was on assignment, I could forget for a while. Every text or email from Wade or Bowie brought it all back. I couldn't face them. And I certainly couldn't tell them the truth."

No, of course not. He couldn't tell Wade and Bowie he'd been in the enemy camp.

"So you stayed away. And all this time, Wade blamed himself?"

"I didn't realize that until recently. Then I recalled some tense things we said in the heat of the moment during those first days while we grappled to make sense of the loss."

"You told him it was his fault?"

"Yeah. Maybe. I don't know. Accusing him of neglecting his duties didn't change the truth. I figured he knew that."

"Does he now?"

"I hope so."

"If you're unsure, why not talk to him, discuss everything and get it all out on the table? Like ripping off a Band-Aid, it may hurt for a minute, but in the long run, you'll both be better." She raised her palms in question. "But what does any of this have to do with Bud Keno?"

"You. He knows we were together that day and has threatened to tell Wade unless I stop seeing you."

"Then what's the problem? Tell Wade first." *Unless you're ashamed of me.*

Was he?

"Don't you get it? The constant antagonism between us and our neighbors is bad enough. I won't drag you, an innocent party, into our messes."

"I don't see your point. If you tell Wade the whole story, Bud has no ammunition."

"You want me to tell my brother, a Trudeau, that you, the town's respected newspaper publisher and a fine Christian woman—who happens to be related to the Keno clan—were secretly sneaking around with a Trudeau on the day his brother was killed?"

She bristled. "You make our relationship sound seedy and dirty. It wasn't." It had been beautiful, at least to her. "The secrecy was ridiculous, but we were young and thought it necessary then. Maybe even thrilling. We didn't want to cause any more trouble between our families."

"We were protecting them." His tone was derisive. "Or so I thought. In the end, I didn't protect anyone. Not Trent. Not you. No one. By keeping my mouth shut now, I can shield you from Keno's innuendoes and your grandmother's anger as well as my brother's."

So this was what had been bugging him all this time? He was protecting her? This was the thing creating a barrier between them?

"Why didn't you tell me this sooner? Really, Yates, you're overreacting. It's much ado about nothing."

"'Overreacting'? My brother died."

"That's not my meaning. I'm talking about my part. Tell the world we were together that day. Take out an ad in the paper. I don't care." And then, because she needed to hear his denial, she said the words that kept circling in her brain over and over again. "Unless you're ashamed of me."

"'Ashamed'? You think that?" He looked completely stunned by her comment. "How could you think that?"

"Well? Are you?" The words trembled from her tongue, pathetic, almost pleading.

"No! No! I want to shield you from the backlash."

Laurel walked into Yates's chest and put her arms around his narrow waist. "I love you for wanting to keep my name out of a bad situation. I do. But I want you to stop. We aren't dumb kids anymore, and I don't care who knows if we dated back then. The secrecy was foolish anyway. That's why I won't allow it anymore."

"Not foolishness. Self-preservation."

"I get that. It's no longer necessary." She tilted her face

toward his. Her heart thundered in her chest. "I don't want this or anything else between us anymore. I care about you, Yates."

"I know." He leaned his forehead against hers. "I care about you too. That's why I want to protect you."

"I don't think you understand." Her heartbeat ratcheted up. It was now or never. "I more than care, Yates. I love you. I've loved you for a long time, even though I convinced myself that I was over you. I tried to be. You were gone. You didn't communicate. What we had was over. But it wasn't. Not really. Not for me. I never stopped praying for you, never stopped wondering if I'd ever see you again, if you ever thought about me."

Laurel heard the ache in her own voice.

She placed a hand alongside Yates's whiskered jaw, wondering if he heard it, too, and if she'd said too much too soon.

But she needed to know where this thing between them was headed.

She'd already wasted too many years.

Yates closed his eyes against the pain on Laurel's face. He'd done that. He'd broken her heart and left her hurting.

"I thought about you all the time," he whispered. "Every single day."

He shouldn't have told her that. He was only making things harder for both of them.

This *thing* between them couldn't go any further than it had already gone.

"Same here, though I tried not to." Her lips curved into a smile, but her eyes still carried sorrow. "Then one day you popped up out of the blackberry bushes, looking like a scrawny Bigfoot, and every wall I'd erected against your memory crumbled at your feet."

He wanted to chuckle at the image, but his throat felt too full.

"Thank you for telling me about Bud and his threats," she said. "I knew something was bothering you, holding you back, but I was beginning to think there was something wrong with me."

"Wrong with you? Never. No. It's me, not you." The problem was his, not hers, and neither of them could do a thing about it.

"But now that you have that off your chest…" She let the thought drift away, but he read her meaning.

Laurel thought the problems keeping them apart were resolved. But she was wrong. And he wasn't about to tell her. Not about his injury. She'd insist that his damaged body and dire future didn't bother her, but it would. In the long run, she'd resent the stress of being strapped to a time bomb.

"You're the finest woman on this planet, Laurel. Special. Beautiful. Caring."

She smiled, and Yates knew he was only making things worse.

"Keep talking, soldier boy."

He shouldn't. But she deserved to know that it wasn't her problem that stood between them.

"There's no one I admire or respect more than you. All the good things you do in this town. For kids, for me. Letting me back in your life when I deserved to be shot on sight. That takes a very special kind of woman."

"Love does that, Yates."

"Yeah." He tried to ease past her monumental declaration, but it lingered in the kitchen, sweeter than the cookie dough.

The words he wanted to speak in reply rose in the back of his throat. He tried to swallow them.

The oven beeped.

A last-second reprieve.

"Cookies are done."

He released her and turned toward the stove.

Chapter Twelve

A half-moon hung over the ranch by the time Yates let himself in through the back door and moved quietly through the kitchen toward his section of the house.

Not wanting to disturb the family, he didn't bother with the house lights. Although the hour wasn't that late, the triplets went to bed early, and the house was necessarily quieter after that.

Accustomed to stealthy movement under cover of darkness, his cell phone's flashlight was more than enough light. Justice must have thought he was on duty, because he began sweeping the room with his incredible nose. Yates let him have his fun.

As he passed the door to the living room, Wade's voice stopped him. "Out late, aren't you?"

Yates paused in the entry, feeling as guilty as a sneaking teenager. "Waiting up for me, *Daddy*?"

Wade, kicked back in a recliner with a book in hand and the lamp next to him burning low, chuckled. "As a matter of fact, I was. Have a seat. We need to talk."

Unease slid over Yates's spine.

Tapping off his flashlight, he settled in the chair opposite his brother. "What's up?"

"I had an interesting phone call right before you came in."

Keno? Please, not him.

Yates swallowed. "And?"

Wade's recliner popped as he sat up straight. "Laurel Maxwell."

Yates's stomach dipped low and fast, the way it did when he jumped from an airplane into hostile territory.

The better part of wisdom said to keep his mouth shut and listen, but he'd never had a lick of sense when it came to Laurel.

"Don't be upset with Laurel. You knew I was spending time with her. It wasn't a secret."

Wrong choice of words.

"It used to be."

"So she told you about that. Long time ago." He maintained his poker face, but his pulse pounded. Had she told his brother everything, even about the day of Trent's death? "What else did she say?"

"She said the two of you were secretly dating eight years ago before you joined the army and that the two of us—" he motioned between them "—needed to talk about something very important."

Hip aching, Yates readjusted his position. "Not that important."

"Look, brother, it took some guts for Laurel to call here. I'd say this must be important. She refused to betray your confidence, but she said it had to do with Trent. She also said she refused to be part of keeping any more secrets concerning the stupid Keno-Trudeau feud. 'Stupid.' Her word."

"She's right."

"So what's the big secret? What does Laurel Maxwell know about our family that I don't? I don't particularly appreciate the names Trent and Keno in the same conversation."

"Me either."

Wade leaned forward, hands clasped between his knees, waiting. "So?"

Yates's stomach churned. "I don't want to talk about this."

"You say that a lot, brother, but maybe it's time to get it out in the open. Whatever this is that's eating at you. You're moody. You don't eat. You roam the countryside like a lost soul."

Yates moved in his chair, restless, the load heavy on him.

Maybe it *was* time. "I don't want to lose you, Wade. Me, you, Bowie, Trent—we were close. I didn't realize the good thing we had until I left. I don't want to destroy everything all over again."

Wade raised one eyebrow. "You're not making a lot of sense, dude."

Yates blew out a breath, tried to calm his spinning brain and assemble all the words he'd kept locked inside for years. "You were not to blame for Trent's accident."

"You've already said that about a hundred times."

"His death was my fault."

"You said that, too, but I never saw how it could be any more yours than mine."

"I was in charge. Worse, and the thing you *don't* know..." Blowing out a long breath, Yates let the harsh truth tumble out. "I gave Trent permission to go to the bull pen alone that day."

Silence dangled like a live grenade in the space between them. He waited for it to explode.

Finally, in a deathly quiet voice, Wade asked the lethal question. "Why?"

"This is on me, not on Laurel. Hit me, despise me, kick me out of the family, but don't lay this at Laurel's door."

Wade stared at him for three long, agonizing beats. "Oh, I see. I get it now. You were with her instead of your little brother."

The sharp dagger of remorse sliced through Yates's heart all over again. Shredded him. "Yeah."

Wade's gaze lasered into him. He bounced clenched

thumbs against his chin. "You actually told Trent he could go to the bull pen alone?"

"One time. Just once. I thought once wouldn't hurt." Choking on the last word, he stopped talking. That one time had not only hurt his entire family—it had taken Trent's life.

A man couldn't explain that away no matter how much he tried.

Wade leaned back in his chair and put his face down against clasped hands and closed his eyes as if in prayer.

Yates had never wanted so badly to believe God was listening. He ached with the need to share his brother's devotion.

The hypersensitive Justice nudged Yates's dangling fingertips and whined softly, offering comfort.

Comfort wouldn't come.

"I'll understand if you want me to move out. I'll sign my share of the ranch over to you and—"

Wade's head popped up. "No! I've lost one brother, and when you disappeared, I thought I'd lost you both. If there's one thing I've learned from Jesus and my incredible wife, it's this—we can't undo the past. We learn from it and try to do better moving forward. With God's help. That's the only way to get through this life with any joy and peace."

Yates's mouth fell open. His brother's declaration circled through his brain, leaving hope and amazement in its wake. "You can forgive me?"

"Holding a grudge is what got us into this mess in the first place. Grudges and secrets are like that."

When did Wade get so wise?

"What about Laurel? I don't want any more hard feelings toward her because of this."

"Your girlfriend is a pretty stand-up lady, calling here the way she did. I respect that. And her honesty."

Yates didn't bother to correct his brother's use of the word "girlfriend." "She's a special woman."

"I think I found that out tonight." Wade shifted in the chair. "Want to tell me how Bud Keno got into this conversation?"

Might as well spill it all and be done with it. Purge the soul and see what happened. "Bud knew that Laurel and I dated secretly. I don't know how he found out, but he knew I was with her the day Trent died."

"Ah." Nodding, Wade tapped his fingers against the arm of the recliner. "And he threatened to tell me."

"He thought it would stir up trouble between you and me."

"He'd love that, wouldn't he?" Wade got an ornery grin on his face. "So let's prove him wrong."

Sometime later, after a long heartfelt talk that left him exhausted but amazingly relieved, Yates lay in his bed, hands stacked behind his head, thinking.

He'd expected an explosion of recriminations and fury from his brother. He'd expected renewed grief and loss. Over Trent's death. About Yates's relationship with Laurel.

What he hadn't expected was a loving response filled with forgiveness and wisdom.

Wade was starting to sound like Dad, especially the gentle reminder that everyone needed Jesus, whether Yates thought he did or not. His little brother had done some serious growing up.

Reaching for the cell phone on his bedside stand, Yates tapped the photo of Laurel's beautiful laughing face. He'd snapped the candid shot when he'd taken her and the Stafford kids fishing at Hidden Pond. Thinking she had snagged a big one, she reeled in a perch the size of a minnow and laughed until the teeny fish escaped back into the water. Then she'd laughed some more.

He loved that picture. And that memory.

The text curser blinked from the blank display, the only light in the room. It was late. She was likely asleep. Why bother her?

But what if she thought he was angry about her phone call to Wade? He didn't want her to worry.

She'd taken a big risk with that call, making herself vulnerable, refusing the protection Yates had tried so hard to give her.

Amazing woman.

He typed in a message.

You asleep?

A minute passed and then, No. Chelsey had a bad dream.

Is she okay?

She is now.

Can I call you? Or is too late?

Call.

Laurel stared at her cell phone, fretting. Was she about to be blasted into outer space by a very angry man?

If so, she wouldn't argue. She'd sown to the wind, and now she'd reap the hurricane.

The call to Wade had been made with the best of intentions. It certainly hadn't been easy, even though Wade Trudeau had been surprisingly polite, if cool.

She had expected worse.

If she'd done a good thing for the brothers, she would be happy. Even if Yates was upset with her.

She prayed that the pair had cleared the air and come together in solidarity. If that solidarity was against her and her blood relatives, she'd be no worse off than before. At least Wade and Yates would be mended. Truth and openness, both in news reporting and life, were essential.

She'd decided to make that call before Yates had even left her house. The man she loved would have a clear conscience and a fresh start with his brother. He needed that, and she wanted it for him.

That's what love did. Even if it cost her another heartache.

The phone in her hand vibrated. She drew in an anxious breath and answered.

"You talked to Wade?" she asked. No greeting. Just get to the point.

"Yes."

She braced for the consequences. They didn't come.

"And you're still speaking to me?"

His breath huffed softly into the phone. "How can I be angry with a woman who took that kind of chance on my behalf? A Keno calling up a Trudeau with less-than-stellar news took some major guts."

"It was scary. I'll admit it."

He chuckled. "Wade's a good guy, Laurel. And you were right. The story needed to come out."

Yates wasn't angry. He was…sweet.

Her heart squeezed. Oh, that man and his complexities—how she loved him.

"How upset is he?" Balancing the phone between shoulder and ear, she settled in the stuffed chair at the foot of her bed and curled her bare feet beneath her.

"He's not. According to Wade, he was stunned to get your call and had to think it through, but by the time I made the drive to the ranch, he had his head together."

"And?"

"And get this. He admires you for making that call."

"Admires *me*?"

"Yeah. Thinks you're a stand-up woman with a lot of integrity. He liked your straightforward honesty. Rip off the bandage, as you say, and let the wound air."

"Wow. I'm...thankful. I think maybe God is doing something here. For you and your family, for us." Couldn't he feel it?

"I figured you were praying. Wade was too."

"Of course I was." God had intervened in what could have been a messy conversation. "I'm a peace-loving girl. I want people to be happy. The Bible says to be at peace as much as you possibly can, even with your enemies. Not that I view your family as enemies."

"I've been wrong about a lot of things, Laurel. Even us."

"'Us'?" Did her voice quiver a little?

"You and me makes an 'us,' doesn't it?"

What was he getting at?

Her pulse picked up. "I suppose it does."

"Okay, good. I'll see you tomorrow after work? Chinese takeout?"

"Tomorrow evening is my Bible-study group."

"Oh."

"Come with me?" She held her breath.

Two beats passed and then three. She braced for his refusal.

"What time?"

Attending a Bible study with Laurel was the least he could do after she'd run the gauntlet with Wade and he had been the beneficiary.

Admittedly, the gathering made him uncomfortable. He'd not attended any sort of religious event in years. Even then, they'd attended different churches.

Bringing the kids along made things easier, and the

study group proved to be casual and friendly. He also knew several of the attendees. Food, friends, lots of laughs and a few gentle—though lively—disagreements over scripture interpretation made for an okay outing.

He figured he could handle anything with Laurel sitting at his side, her smile bright every time she looked his way. Which was often.

During the teaching, Yates said little but figured no one expected a guest to share much input. He listened, though.

After the lesson, which didn't bother him as much as he'd expected, Laurel nudged him. "Want to go out in the backyard with the kids and challenge me in cornhole?"

"Are you any good?"

Laughing, she grabbed his hand. "Come and see."

Yates allowed Laurel to tug him through the patio doors into the backyard, where kids ran amok and a hot game of cornhole, complete with joking insults, was in progress.

From the far corner of the long, fenced yard, Megan and Chelsey spotted them and broke into a run, faces aglow with delight. Megan's much shorter legs couldn't keep pace. She stumbled and went down.

Laurel released his hand and bolted toward the fallen child. Yates followed at a considerably slower pace but as quickly as he could move.

Before he reached them, Laurel was crouched next to the little girl, wiping grass and dirt from Megan's hands. Then she placed a sweet kiss on each palm.

"All better?"

Yeah, he was. Although he knew she was speaking to Megan, Laurel Maxwell also spoke to his heart. Being with her made him better too.

There. He'd admitted it. At least to himself. He needed Laurel in his life. With Bud Keno's threats out of the picture, the decision was his to make.

He had been wrong about so many things. Was he

wrong not to tell this incredible woman about the shrapnel? He could guess what she would say if she knew. She would tell him it didn't matter.

Was it fair to her, though? That was his dilemma. He loved her, wanted to do right by her.

He reached her side and, after commiserating with Megan's boo-boo, he extended a hand to Laurel and helped her stand.

She smiled up at him and said, "Disaster averted."

Yes, Megan's disaster was averted.

But what about his?

Did he dare hope the worst would never happen? Did he dare believe he could live a healthy life and never be a burden to anyone he loved?

He'd thought he could live out the rest of his days aloof, alone, self-contained, without the love a woman.

But he hadn't reckoned on Laurel Maxwell.

"You're happy this morning." Tansy slid a banana-nut muffin onto Laurel's desk. "I could hear you humming when I came in the door."

"Things are looking up. Subscriptions have mysteriously risen, and the reaction from readers to our experiment of printing more local news and events has proven stunningly enthusiastic."

Tansy grinned her Cheshire cat smile. "Told you."

Laurel pinched off a bite of fragrant, still-warm muffin. "Not true. You hated the idea because Yates thought of it first."

"Did not."

"Did too."

They both laughed.

Laurel motioned toward the muffin. "Is this your bakery treat for the day? No doughnuts?"

"I'm being more health-conscious. At least once a week."

"They're good." She smiled and enjoyed another bite. The banana flavor, coupled with spice and vanilla, burst on her tongue, satisfying. "If this is health food, sign me up."

"It's a start. Not fried dough, anyway." Tansy hitched a hip against the edge of Laurel's desk. Today's T-shirt proclaimed, *I got lost in thought. It was unfamiliar territory.*

"He makes you happy."

"Who?" Warmth rose up Laurel's neck and into her cheeks.

"Don't play coy. You haven't hummed and sung around this office in—" Tansy waved dramatically, searching for the right word "—forever. Not since before Yates went away."

Laurel pushed her computer monitor to one side and folded both arms on top of her desk.

With a sigh, she admitted, "I love him, Tansy. I always have."

"I know." Instead of the lecture Laurel had expected, Tansy nodded. "What are you going to do about him?"

"I don't know. See where the relationship takes us, I suppose."

"What about Yates? How does he feel? Or is he messing with your heart again? Because if he is, I'll kneecap him myself. I own a baseball bat, you know."

Laurel laughed. "Tough girl. You and Yates both fight to look out for me, but I'm pretty sure I can handle myself this time."

"You didn't answer my question. You're in love, but what about him?"

"Are you saying I'm unlovable?"

"Not even close. If the man has a lick of sense, which I've always doubted, he'll be on his knees, begging you to marry him."

"I like that image."

"So has he admitted he's crazy about you yet or not?"

"In actions, yes—and he says he cares for me. With Yates, that's a big step. I'm pretty confident he loves me."

"What will Grandma say?"

Laurel grimaced. "She's not happy. Whenever he comes to the house, which is nearly every night unless I'm at his place, Gran takes to her room and refuses to come out until he leaves. We ignore her, but I feel bad for both of them. Her rudeness is embarrassing. And needless."

"If she knew about what happened before, she'd never let him past the front step."

"True. But he's different now." At least, she hoped he was. He was still private and so controlled, keeping his emotions locked inside, that she worried about him. Since talking to Wade about Trent's death and Bud Keno's threats, he had lightened up some.

Just not enough.

He loved her. She was sure of it.

Yet something still bothered him. She just wished she knew what it was.

Chapter Thirteen

Yates awakened from the best dream of his life. Better yet, the dream was becoming reality.

The two of them, he and Laurel, were at someone's wedding, and suddenly that wedding was theirs. Laurel was in a long, white lacy dress, her blond hair shining beneath a sheer veil and her golden eyes holding his with enough love to start a forest fire.

Her beauty, inside and out, filled his chest with pleasure.

Standing beside her, he'd seen himself as healthy and strong, his body fit—the way he'd been before the blast. Gone was the fear that he could never be the man she deserved.

Keeping his eyes closed, though now fully awake, Yates stacked his hands behind his head and relived the perfect dream in his mind.

He'd been fooling himself that he could be her friend and not fall madly in love with her again.

Would she marry him?

His lips curved. She would. He knew it.

He wouldn't ask yet. But maybe soon. When he'd regained more of his weight and had his strength back to one hundred percent. When his body was as healed as it could ever be.

The thoughts that he would never completely heal, that he would always carry in his body the threat of paralysis, tried to push in.

He blocked them.

He'd beat this thing. He'd be okay. He had to be. For Laurel.

"Time to get up."

When Yates spoke, Justice rose from his dog bed, shook out his fur and ambled over to his bedside.

Yates trailed a hand over the dog's ears. "Got work to do today, boy. You, me, the horses. I'm feeling good. We'll work out the mares and Excalibur, then drive the tractor out to pasture three with the fertilizer." Wade had asked last night if he was up to the fieldwork. He thought he was.

Stretching his arms up over his head, he yawned, feeling good, thinking positive.

He grinned a little as he thought about Excalibur, the beautiful stallion Bud Keno coveted. He actually looked forward to another, much more satisfying, confrontation with the man. This time, he'd tell Bud exactly what he could do with his mean-spirited attitude. Now that Wade and Laurel knew the truth about that awful day of Trent's death, Excalibur wasn't going anywhere.

The grin widened. Neither were he or Laurel.

As he'd been taught in physical therapy, he rolled to one side to lever up without putting undue strain on his back.

His legs tingled.

No big deal. Don't panic. Must have slept crooked.

Except that he hadn't.

He swallowed hard, took a deep breath and tried to swing his sweats-clad legs over the side.

They didn't cooperate.

His breathing increased. Beads of sweat prickled the back of his neck. His pulse picked up, pounded against his collarbone.

"Come on. Come on."

He tried again, straining to move, willing his body to

cooperate. His legs tingled worse, pins and needles, as if they'd gone to sleep and couldn't wake up.

That's all it was. All it could be. Like when he was a kid and sat with his legs curled beneath him too long. They'd wake up in a minute or two.

Please.

Reaching down, he clasped first one knee and then the other, swinging his legs off the bed.

They dangled there, tingling, numb, unresponsive.

Fear hammered a hole in his brain. Stole his breath. Choked him.

He wasn't afraid of much. This terrified him.

Crippled, helpless, unable to care for himself.

Yates Trudeau depended on no one. Ever.

He was a man whose athletic body and masculine strength defined him. As a soldier, as a cowboy, as a man. He was useless without his mobility. Wasn't he?

How could he bear this?

For several long minutes, Yates sat on the edge of the bed, panting, wishing he could pray but certain he'd waited too long. God wouldn't answer a selfish prayer when a man had ignored Him for years.

Mouth dry, sweat dampening his T-shirt, Yates heard the harsh sound of his own breathing in the quiet room.

Justice nudged his dangling foot.

Yates glanced down. Blinked. Frowned.

Had he felt that?

He squeezed one kneecap. Then the other.

Relief flooded through him. Moisture seeped beneath his eyelids.

He could feel. He squeezed harder, pushing deep to cause pain. Through the tingling, the squeeze hurt.

Almost shouting with joy, he squeezed again. Pain was better than nothingness.

He wasn't paralyzed. Yet.

But the shrapnel had let him know, had warned him.

Don't dream too much. Don't want too much.

Don't even think about putting Laurel in the position of having to care for an invalid husband.

Laurel dropped the children off at school after an early-morning visit with their father.

"Bye, Laurel." Waving hands joined the chorus of three voices.

Schoolbag bobbing against her tiny shoulders, Megan raced back to the car. "I love you. Bye."

"Love you, too, sweet pea," Laurel managed around the lump in her throat. "Have a great day."

Megan nodded, all smiles. "'Be Jesus to the world.' That's what Daddy says."

"He's right. I know you will make him proud. Bye now."

The dark-haired preschooler, red ribbons flying, rushed to catch up with her sister and brother.

Laurel had grown accustomed to seeing those three shining faces every morning. Through the Big Sister program, she'd already been close to them. Now she was attached like Velcro.

How would she feel when they left Sundown Valley for good?

She'd allowed them to become the children she always wanted, and though saying goodbye would hurt, she didn't regret loving them. They'd needed her. Taking them into her home had been the right thing to do. The thing God had asked of her.

Caring for them wasn't about her or her longing for children of her own. Her feelings didn't matter. Not in this instance.

Doing right by the children was the important thing.

But oh, she dreamed of a family of her own.

Laurel took a sip from her travel mug and watched until her charges disappeared inside the school building.

Stephen's sister planned to leave Thailand by the end of the month. That was only three weeks away.

She swallowed the warm coffee to wash down the bittersweet emotion bubbling in her throat.

Would their aunt know their favorite foods or that Aiden needed extra help with reading? Or that Chelsey sometimes had bad dreams and needed to snuggle until she fell asleep again?

All these things ran through Laurel's mind as she put the car in drive and slowly pulled away from the mass of vehicles and people flooding the school.

As she reached the newspaper office and parked around back, her cell phone chirped. Yates's name appeared on her car's Bluetooth screen.

Pleasure curled beneath her rib cage. Yates called first thing every morning and last thing at night, even after they'd been together.

Sometimes they talked for hours more. Hearing his voice, knowing he was back in her life, was more important to her than the extra sleep.

After putting the car in park and killing the engine, she fished the cell phone from her purse and tapped the screen.

As she read the text, disappointment dampened her happy mood. He was breaking tonight's date. No excuse, no reason. Just that he couldn't make it.

Her thumbs danced over the keyboard. Is everything okay?

Busy at the ranch. Take care.

Take care? What did that mean? He never signed off that way.

Oh well. She was being insecure and reading more into

the vague text than was there. They'd talk by phone tonight and everything would be fine.

It wasn't. In fact, Yates didn't call at all. So she called him. The conversation was short, terse. He was busy.

By the end of the week, she knew something was wrong. Being a bull-by-the-horns kind of gal, Laurel chose the direct route. Face-to-face.

She waited until Friday night, after the children were in bed and Gran had agreed to keep an eye on them.

"Where are you gallivanting off to at this hour?" Gran demanded in her equally no-nonsense manner.

"To see Yates."

Gran bristled, as Laurel had expected, but she refused to skirt the issue any longer. She was dating Yates, and that was that. More than dating. They were a couple. In love.

The notion gave her a happy shiver and the courage to stand up to her grandmother.

One hand to her hip, Gran glared at her for a long moment. Finally, she huffed and said, "At least put on some lipstick."

Laurel choked back the laugh of surprise. "I love you, Gran."

"Go on with you." Gran flustered was a sight to see.

Laurel dutifully put on some lipstick, got in her car and headed to the Sundown Ranch.

"Yates, you've got company." Kyra's voice came through his bedroom door. He'd been in no mood for company tonight—not family or otherwise.

"Who is it?"

"Come see for yourself."

With a sigh of annoyance, Yates set his laptop aside and pushed out of the chair he'd dragged into the guest room for reading and computer work. Wade had turned some of the bookwork over to him—whether out of the actual need for office help or because of pity, he couldn't say, but the work gave him purpose.

Exiting the room, he traversed the long hallway from the north bedrooms to the front of the house. As he entered the foyer, his stomach dropped.

"Laurel?"

Kyra's gaze bounced between them. She must have noticed the tension, because she said, "I'll leave you two to visit. The living room is empty, if you want to go in there."

After his sister-in-law disappeared around the corner, Yates motioned toward the front door. "I'd rather talk outside. Let's walk."

He hadn't expected this visit, but maybe he should have. Laurel wasn't the compliant young woman she'd been eight years ago. She was strong, standing up for herself as well as others. It was one of the many traits he admired; although at the moment, her purposeful, forthright attitude was problematic.

Holding the door while Laurel passed through, Yates followed her across the porch and onto the driveway leading in various directions from the house.

His thoughts raced as he tried to think of the right words. How did he tell her goodbye when he wanted to be with her forever?

Yet this wasn't about what he wanted. Laurel's future was at stake. If he loved her, he would let her go.

He had to remember that.

Security lights illuminated their path, though long shadows stretched between and around them. A whip-poor-will cried from somewhere in the woods. Yates felt the mournful sound all the way to his marrow.

This would not be an easy conversation. He kept quiet, waiting for her to lead. If he wasn't careful, he'd blurt the exact opposite of what he knew he must say.

The soft night sounds closed around them. He could hear the pounding of his own heart and wished with all his might to be in some dangerous terrorist camp half a world away.

He was not a coward. A fool, perhaps, but not a coward.

"You want to tell me what's going on?" Laurel asked as they walked side by side, not touching, though he wanted badly to gather her close and forget about his broken body. "Why have you suddenly turned as cold as January and stopped talking to me?"

The worry in her voice jabbed at him.

He had to do the right thing. He had to release her. Holding on when they were hopeless would only cause her more heartache in the long run.

"I've been putting off this conversation," he admitted quietly, speaking into the shadows, avoiding her probing gaze. "I'm trying to figure out what to say, how to say it."

"You're scaring me."

"I'm sorry."

Putting a hand on his arm, Laurel stopped his forward progress.

He fought off the longing to embrace her.

Laurel had no such misgivings. Stepping close, she put her arms around his waist. Yates stood like a good soldier, arms at his side, drawing on his training to remain in control.

If he held her and felt the beat of her heart against his, scented her sweet fragrance, touched her soft skin, he might lose his nerve and crumble.

Head tilted back to look at him, Laurel was gilded by moonlight. So beautiful. So inaccessible. To him, at least.

"I love you, Yates. Whatever is wrong, we can talk about it, fix it. Together."

This was what he'd been dreading. The ache in her

voice and the knowledge that he would have to hurt her to set her free.

"Some things can't be fixed, Laurel."

"Try me." She cupped the side of his whiskered jaw, forcing him to look into her true and honest eyes.

He fought the urgent desire to kiss her and to pretend that all was well, that they could be together.

But that was unfair to her.

With all the courage he possessed—and he'd needed plenty in the army—he expanded his chest with a deep inhale and slowly let the air seep out.

"Laurel," he began, his throat rusty with emotion, "you're the most incredible woman I've ever known. Beautiful, smart, kind, strong and more." *Say it, be done with it and let her go.* "I'm sorry, so sorry, to have led you on, but we aren't right for each other."

He felt her stiffen, saw her tender, loving expression melt into pained confusion.

The need to touch her tormented him.

He resisted. For her, he could remain detached—a soldier doing his duty. Fulfill the assignment and get out.

"I don't understand." Her voice quavered. "I thought we were—you said—I thought you loved me."

He did. Oh, he did. He loved her too much to saddle her with his broken self. Yet if he told her that much, he'd have to say the rest. Better to let her believe the worst about him than to watch her love turn to pity and obligation. To sentence her to life with him.

Yates stepped away from her, watched her arms fall to her sides. If he let her go on embracing him, he couldn't set her free.

As it was, he waged an epic battle not to crush her to his chest and beg her never to leave. To tell her how scared he was sometimes of the future. To declare how much he needed her.

"It's time to cut our losses now and move on with our lives."

"No." The sorrow in that one word nearly drove him to his knees.

She reached a hand toward him.

He closed his eyes against her.

Speaking the words he'd rehearsed all week, he said, "Go find the man you deserve, Laurel. Get married, have that houseful of kids. Just not with me."

"I don't understand this. Last week, we were moving toward forever, and now you don't want to see me anymore? Was it my grandma? Or one of the Kenos? Did they do this?"

"I simply woke up one morning and realized you need and deserve something I can't give you." A true statement, if ever he'd spoken one.

Her shoulders slumped. In a quiet, throbbing voice, she said, "So it's true, then, what Tansy said all along."

"What?"

"That you only dated me to prove a Trudeau could make a Keno fall in love with him. Was that true? Was that the reason for the secrecy back then and the breakup now? Some kind of cruel game you Trudeau men play?"

Her voice rose in what he hoped was anger. Better an angry Laurel than a heartbroken one.

What could he say? There was an element of truth in the accusation. Not much, but a tiny particle.

Let her think the worst. Let her hate him, though her loathing would rip him into more shreds than the mortar blast.

"Yes."

She sucked in a wounded gasp. "All that time, you lied to me?"

Only in the beginning. After he'd gotten to know her even the slightest amount, he'd been swamped with feelings of guilt and stronger feelings of love. Laurel was not a game to him.

Now was not the time to admit that knowing her had changed him.

"Trudeaus and Kenos don't go together. You knew that from the beginning. So did I. There's nothing left to say except goodbye." He dipped his head in a curt nod. "I'll walk you to your car."

Laurel pressed her fingers to her mouth and turned to the side. In the dim light, tears shone on her cheeks.

She was killing him.

And he deserved it.

"I have been such a fool." Spinning around, she held her head high and walked toward the car.

Yates struggled to keep pace. His slow, awkward gait served as a reminder that setting her free was the right thing.

He opened the driver's door for her, and she slid inside. Without looking at him, she started the engine.

"Shut the door," she demanded. But at the last second, she glanced up. Her eyes swam with tears. "I love you, Yates."

He closed the door, turned his back and continued toward the house.

She'd gutted him with that parting shot. She loved him, in spite of the ugly things he'd said.

As her car motored down the driveway, he stood in the shadows of the porch and watched until the red taillights disappeared.

When he could see her no more, he whispered into the night.

"I love you, too, Laurel Maxwell. I always will."

The knock sounded on Laurel's bedroom door with more intensity this time.

"I'm coming in, Laurel. Get decent."

Gran had seen her enter the house after the awful confrontation with Yates. She had seen the tears.

"I don't want to talk. It's late."

"Not that late, young lady." The knob turned and Gran, toting her oxygen like armor, marched inside. "What did he do? That Trudeau boy. He's done something. I know it. First, he doesn't show his ugly face around here for a week, then you run off to see him, and now you're crying behind closed doors."

After that long tirade, Gran panted for air.

"We broke up."

"Those swollen eyes mean *he* did the breaking."

"Yes." Her nose was so stopped up the word came out as "yeth."

"That's what Trudeau men do. They make women fall in love with them and then leave them stranded."

"I'm not stranded. And this has nothing to do with him being a Trudeau." Except it sort of did. After all, he'd dated her to prove a Trudeau could make a Keno fall in love with him.

She believed him. And yet, she didn't.

He loved her. She was sure of it.

Tears pushed to the fore again.

Was she that pathetic that she couldn't accept rejection?

Gran plopped down on the edge of the bed. "Good riddance to rubbish, if you ask me. He doesn't deserve you."

"That's what he said."

Gran blinked at her, owl-eyed. "He did? That doesn't sound like a Trudeau."

Tears leaked out the corners of Laurel's eyes and slithered down her cheeks. "He's a good man. I believe he loves me, but something's holding him back. Something he won't talk about."

"Don't lie to yourself, girl. A man like that loves only himself. He's a user."

He wasn't, and the need to defend him, even now, rose fiercely in Laurel. She bit back the reply. What good would arguing do?

Gran huffed. "And to think he was starting to grow on me."

Laurel sniffed, dabbed at her leaky eyes. "He was?"

"Which proves I'm becoming a doddering old lady without a lick of sense."

"Not true. You finally saw who he really is." Laurel reached for another tissue. "And maybe you recognize the harm in carrying a grudge. The Bible tells us not to do that. If we have a problem with someone, go to them and work it out."

Gran pointed a finger at her stuffy nose. "Don't preach to me, young lady. I'm as good a Christian as anyone. I just refuse to like a family who hurts mine. We Kenos defend our own."

Laurel put a hand on her grandma's arm. Gran loved her. That's why she was angry at Yates.

"Of course we do. All families do. But as long as I've known them, the Trudeaus have never done anything to hurt us."

Gran emitted a derisive sound. "Perhaps not in this generation…"

Sitting cross-legged, Laurel faced Gran. For years, she'd wondered. "What happened to convince you that all Trudeaus are evil? Do you know what started the grudge?"

"I do. At least, the story my grandmother told me." Gran rested a minute to catch her breath, her sharp gaze searching Laurel's. "You're old enough now to hear it, I suppose, though my granny claimed the shame was too great to pass on."

"Yet she told you."

Humor wrinkled Gran's face. "I was as persistent a gnat as you."

"Could something really be that shameful, and so terrible, that generations continue to harbor deep resentment and animosity? It isn't right, Gran."

"You aren't the first Keno woman to fall for a Trudeau man. The story is tragic. Are you sure you want to hear it?"

"Absolutely." Clear the air, rip off the bandage. Isn't that what she'd said to Yates?

"It happened a long time ago. My grandma's great-aunt, if I have story the straight after all this time, fell for a Trudeau man. She got—" Gran looked to one side and cleared her throat, her always-rosy cheeks deepening in a flush "—in a family way. When he found out, her lover ran away and left her to face the consequences alone."

Laurel scowled in disbelief and surprise. Gran always had difficulty speaking about personal issues. Telling Laurel about the birds and bees had nearly given her apoplexy. But, right or wrong, out-of-wedlock pregnancy was so common today, why keep the secret now?

"That's it? *That* one thing caused years of hostility?"

"No. There's more. The story gets worse." Gran puffed in a few breaths of fresh oxygen. "Remember, now, this happened during a time when bearing a child on the wrong side of the blanket was shameful, unacceptable, a black mark on a family's good name. Although they lied to everyone and said she was away visiting a sick aunt, her parents sent the poor girl to an unwed mothers' home to have the baby and forced her to put it up for adoption. Losing both her love and her baby broke the girl. She never got over the losses."

"What happened to her?"

"Eventually, she returned home. Fearful that she'd repeat her shameful behavior, her family kept her secluded on the farm for the rest of her life. She never left home again. No one even knows when she died. Some say she hung herself."

Laurel touched her fingers to her lips. "Oh, Gran, how awful. That poor girl."

"Exactly. Since then, the two families have despised each other."

"But why? The boy should have stepped up and been responsible, but her family is at fault too. They should have treated her with compassion and forgiveness, not locked her away like a criminal."

Gran sat back, catching her breath, her expression thoughtful. When she spoke again, her words surprised Laurel. "Such was the way of the world back then. But yes, fault existed on both sides."

She patted Laurel on the knee. "I'll ponder this more. But right now, this old lady needs some sleep. Those children will be waking the dead early enough with Megan's cheerful singing and Chelsey's giggles."

She said the last as if the laughter and singing annoyed her. Laurel knew it did not.

"I'll miss them when they leave," Laurel said.

"I won't miss the frogs and worms that Aiden parades into the house from my garden as if he's discovered buried treasure."

Laurel chuckled. "Yes, you will."

Gran snorted and started toward the door.

One hand on the knob, she looked back at Laurel. "If it's any consolation, that Trudeau boy is in love with you. Like all men, he's an idiot, but give him time. He'll come around."

Laurel wished she could believe that.

Chapter Fourteen

Between the dog and his own fine-tuned instincts, Yates heard the two men coming through the woods long before they found him.

He was still good at being invisible.

Without looking up, he said, "Don't sign up to be an army scout. You'd be dead before you moved three feet."

Wade stood over him, his stance wide. "You're the only one who feels the need to hide."

For the past two weeks, he'd not been good company, so he kept to himself.

"Not hiding."

"Then what are you doing out here alone? Again."

"Fishing."

"You're not fishing. You're leaning on a tree trunk."

Yates tensed up for what he knew would be a confrontation he wasn't ready for. "Taking a break. Fish aren't biting."

Wade went to his haunches in front of Yates. The cowboy hat shaded his face, but Yates knew if he looked close enough, he'd see worry.

He didn't like causing worry and was rethinking his decision to come home. He certainly hadn't been any good to anyone. Maybe he should move on. Somewhere. He had some army buddies in Santa Fe.

"You're taking a lot of breaks recently. Alone. Without us, without Aiden. And we've noticed Laurel isn't coming around anymore and you haven't been to town to see her in weeks."

Two. Two long, miserable weeks without Laurel.

Being alone in the wilderness usually cleared his head and brought some measure of peace.

Not this time. He kept having the same two thoughts: Pray. Call Laurel.

He couldn't see a useful purpose in doing either.

His back against the sycamore, Bowie slid down beside Yates. His leather-and-green-grass scent came with him. "What's going on, cuz? You and Laurel break things off?"

Yates plucked a stem of straw.

"Yeah." Maybe that would put an end to their questions.

"Why? You care about her. Any idiot can see that. Even Wade."

Wade laughed at the almost-insult. "He's right. Why would you break up? Even I've started to like her."

"I don't want to have this conversation."

Wade shrugged. "Too bad."

"Here we go again," Bowie murmured.

Looking from the brother in front of him to the cousin beside him, Yates sighed. "You two keeping tabs on me or something?"

"Looks like we need to," Wade said. "You've stopped seeing Laurel and started disappearing on us again—hiding out in the woods, in the barn, in your bedroom."

"I'm fine."

"You're not." Wade's tone darkened, edgy. "We aren't leaving until you talk, so spill it."

"Nothing to say."

"That's a lie."

Yates bristled. "I don't take kindly to being called a liar."

Wade huffed. "You never did. Remember the time you busted my lip?"

Yates grunted. "Dad tanned my hide for it too."

"Bust my lip again if you want to," Wade said, "but you're not shooting straight with us. We recognize avoidance when we see it. That's why Bowie and I are here when we ought to be out cutting hay."

"Yeah, well, I'm pretty worthless in that regard, so you'd better get back to it."

Bowie yanked a handful of grass and sifted it between his fingers. "We love you, man. We'd do anything in the world for you."

Emotion bubbled up like soda pop in Yates's throat. "I know it. I feel the same."

Which was why he couldn't share his health fears.

"Is that the problem? You don't want to upset us about whatever it is that's eating you alive?"

Bowie was too perceptive, and their interrogation was beginning to annoy him. "Why don't you two junior psychologists get back to the ranch and leave me alone? Let me work things out by myself."

"Not happening." Bowie drew his knees up and draped both arms over them as if he was settling in for the day. "If you could handle this alone, you'd have done it by now. Instead, you're getting worse."

Wade dragged over a log, turned it up on one end and sat. His face displayed the same stubborn expression. "No one's leaving here until you tell us what's going on."

Yates's mouth twisted in disgust. "I hope you packed a lunch."

Bowie patted his pocket. "Peanuts. Want some?"

"No. I want you to go away." He jerked his cap from his head and slapped it against his thigh. "What is this, some kind of intervention?"

Wade and Bowie answered in stereo. "Yes."

Yates tilted his head back against the rough bark and sucked fresh air through his nose. What was he going to do now? Sit here and rot while Wade and Bowie stared at him?

His brother could be a firebrand, and when he set his mind to something, nothing moved him. Bowie had always been quietly resolute. They were like two tree stumps: rooted in and determined.

If these two guys loved a person, they'd go to the wall for him, climb over it and defeat the dragons.

"You can't slay this dragon for me, boys."

Had he said that out loud?

"So there *is* a dragon," Bowie said.

Yates looked up to find two intense pair of eyes focused on him—one blue set, one pair of brown. Eyes of love.

"Let us at least try. We're family. If we can't help you—"

"—no one can," Yates interrupted. Frustration tightened a knot in his gut. "Don't you get it? No one can fix this. Not me, not you, not Laurel, not even the doctors."

He lurched away from the tree and, in his embarrassingly awkward manner, pushed to a stand.

Two strong, athletic cowboys came up with him, one on each side, bracketing him when he wobbled like a toddler.

He hated this weakness. *He* was supposed to be the strong one.

"Doctors can't fix you?" Wade had heard what he hadn't intended to blurt.

Yates hung his head, blew out a breath and tried to calm down. He'd said too much. "No. They can't."

"Fix what?" Bowie asked as he settled the Stetson on his dark hair. "We both figured there was more to this injury story than you were saying. The cat's out of the bag. Might as well tell us everything."

"I don't want you to know. I don't anyone to know. I hate pity."

Wade's face darkened. "You won't get it from us."

Yes, he would. They were cowboys who'd talk tough, but they would secretly feel sorry for him. They already talked behind his back. How much worse would it be if they knew he could end up an invalid?

To regain his balance, Yates leaned forward and placed both hands on the tree trunk, head hung low so he wouldn't have to look at their sympathetic faces.

He was so tired of fighting this inward battle. So exhausted from the constant worry and from wishing he could be the man they and Laurel remembered.

A strong hand, light and easy, came to rest against his bony back. Bowie's touch—a hand that could gentle a horse or create intricate designs in leather.

Or comfort his troubled cousin.

"The blast did more damage than you've told us. Right?"

Yates heaved in a gulp of fresh air and let it slowly leak out.

Surrender wasn't in his vocabulary, but this wasn't the military, and these guys weren't the enemy.

What lurked in his spine was the enemy.

Bowie and Wade knew something serious was wrong, and they'd badger him until they knew everything. Trudeaus were a relentless, determined lot.

Pushing away from the tree and the comfort of his cousin's touch, he stared into the green wilderness. Blackberry blooms and wild plum dotted the landscape with white laced among the green and brown.

"I didn't want to worry you."

This time Wade's tone was gentle. "Too late."

Yeah, it was. They'd worry just as much not knowing as they would if he told them.

He sighed. Surrendered. "Docs couldn't get all the shrapnel."

Maybe they wouldn't ask for details.

Bowie was an artist. Detail was his life. So, of course, he asked, "Where?"

Still bracing one hand on the cottonwood, he bent down

to retrieve his fishing pole, though fishing was the last thing on his mind. Justice, feeling his angst, pressed close to his leg.

"My spine. Too close to the spinal cord. If they'd tried to remove it, they could have—"

Voice quiet as a grave, Wade finished the sentence. "Paralyzed you."

Yates glanced up at his brother. The sympathy he'd dreaded shone in the other man's face, along with fear.

Wade was afraid for him.

The notion twisted inside Yates like a living thing.

"Yeah."

"But you're okay, right?" Wade asked hopefully, as if saying he was okay made it so. "You can walk and move. Maybe you're a tad wobbly and slow but better than when you first came home."

"Listen to what he didn't say, Wade." Bowie's wise brown gaze moved from Wade to Yates. "There's still a chance of it, isn't there? Of paralysis?"

Yates licked his dry lips and swallowed. "Yeah."

"Man." Wade's hand clamped onto his shoulder.

Bowie's hand found the other shoulder.

Yates dropped the rod and reel.

These two men loved him more than he loved himself. Stalwart. Strong. Loyal.

Like Laurel.

His throat clogged with emotion. His eyes burned.

"We're here for you, brother. No matter what happens, you have us."

He shook his head. "I won't saddle you with an invalid to care for."

"Let's cross that bridge if we come to it. Maybe we never will." Bowie spoke with quiet confidence. "The important thing to remember is what your dad and mom taught us. Come what may, Jesus will be at your side, walking through this with you. If you'll let Him."

If he'd let Him. Was that the problem? He'd cut God off, pushed Him away, when he should have run toward Him?

"Bow your stubborn head," Wade said, his strong hand squeezing tighter on Yates's shoulder. "We're going to pray."

His heart bursting with emotions he couldn't put into words, he bowed his head and hoped with all his might that God was listening.

They'd kidnapped him.

Yates sat wedged in the back seat of Bowie's pickup truck on his way to somewhere that was bound to upset him. Otherwise they'd tell him where they were going.

"No use trying to hold me for ransom," he said, half-joking and half-annoyed. "My brother won't pay it."

"The cheapskate," Bowie shot from the driver's seat.

Wade, in the front passenger seat, laughed. "Trust me."

Yates snorted. "Said the devil to Eve in the garden."

Wade laughed again.

"Just tell me where we're going."

"Why?" His cousin shot the question over one shoulder. "You got a date?"

"You know better."

"When are you going to give up and talk to her about all this?"

"Who?"

Wade groaned and, in a loud aside to Bowie, commented, "Maybe we should dump him over the river bridge."

"And foul the water? Nah. I like to catfish down there. Yates just needs to come off his high horse and talk to Laurel."

Yates leaned forward in the seat. "I'm not discussing her."

"True. So we are. You're letting your pride stand in the way of doing the right thing."

"The right thing is to keep her out of my life."

"How does she feel about that?" his brother asked, and then, "Oh, that's right. You haven't told her. She thinks you don't care about her."

"I don't."

Wade shifted in the seat to glare at him. "Look me in the face and say that again."

Yates looked down at his knobby-fingered hands.

"That's what I thought." Wade's words poked at him. "You can't look me in the face because you're in love with her. Probably always have been, and you're too hardheaded to do anything about it."

"If I love her—and I'm not saying I do—I won't saddle her with an unknown future."

"Everyone has an unknown future." Bowie's soft voice seemed loud inside the truck cab.

His brother and cousin hammered that phrase into his head, and it was true. No one knew what tomorrow held. No one. But Yates figured a man should control what he could. If he couldn't do anything else, he could protect Laurel from himself.

He shifted uncomfortably and readjusted his seat belt. Wade and Bowie had commandeered him into the back seat, threatening to wrangle him like a calf if he didn't co-operate. Given their frustratingly superior physiques, he'd grudgingly relented. But the smaller back seat proved less than relaxing to his long, thin body.

"I'm asking you to drop the subject of Laurel."

"We could have a little chat with her. Let her know what's going on."

"Don't." The word came out sharp. "Promise me you won't do that. This is my decision."

Wade raised his hands. "All right. All right. The ball is in your court. You have my word."

Bowie glanced in the rearview mirror. "But if you change your mind…"

"I won't."

By now they'd apparently reached their destination. Bowie parked the big four-wheel drive in a lot outside the community center. Other vehicles filled the parking area.

"What's going on? A ball game?"

"Yep. Basketball."

So why had they strong-armed him into coming? He loved basketball.

The moment they walked into the gymnasium, he had his answer.

He pivoted as if to leave. Wade caught his sleeve. "Humor us."

With a heavy sigh and a glare intended to let his brother know exactly how he felt, he relented.

"I'm not paying."

Bowie snickered and withdrew his wallet to purchase the tickets.

Like a condemned prisoner, Yates trailed his captors onto the fold-down bleachers.

"These seats okay?" Wade motioned to a space on the lower level.

"Fine," he growled. His brother instinctively knew stairs were still a challenge. He hated that.

They settled in and the men's game, already in progress, continued. At first, Yates struggled to watch; but soon, he was caught up in the game and in admiring the athletes—every one of them in wheelchairs.

They competed in specially designed chairs with wider wheelbases and secure straps across their laps, but these were not men to pity. They competed hard, fast and with stunning athleticism. Quick, nimble hands dribbled and passed while chairs spun this way and that, blocking, guarding, finding an open lane.

He was impressed.

Fierce competition interspersed with laughter, calls for the ball and the occasional whistle kept the game moving at a pace he hadn't expected.

When the buzzer echoed through the gym, ending the game, Yates was surprised at how quickly the time had passed and how caught up he'd been in the sport.

The athletes, sweat pouring, wheeled to the sidelines, jostling and joking with one another. They grabbed towels and water bottles and formed circles to hear from their coaches.

One group bowed their heads in a silent prayer that brought a lump to Yates's throat. When it ended, fans thundered down from the bleachers, their steps echoing loudly in the cavernous space.

Noise and sweat and competitive fun. Basketball. Different but the same.

He'd known about adaptive sports but had paid them little attention. Until now.

He watched intently as families surrounded the men. Most, he noted, were near his age or younger, with girlfriends or wives and children.

One pretty brunette leaned in and kissed a sweaty, handsome basketball player while a small boy climbed onto his lap.

The scene was repeated more than once. Men in chairs living their lives. Married, with children, playing sports.

Rehab therapists had told him such things were possible, but for him, the idea of dependency was too awful to contemplate. He'd barely listened.

But these men didn't seem dependent. Not at all.

Was God trying to tell him something?

Part of him wanted to pray and seek the peace Bowie

and Wade talked about all the time. God, they claimed, could settle his heart and his fears with a peace beyond human understanding. A peace that trusted in Someone other than himself.

Intellectually, in his problem-solving brain, he couldn't grasp the concept. But maybe that was the point.

God's ways were different. He was more about faith than intellect.

Something to ponder, for certain.

Chapter Fifteen

"Extra, extra," Tansy called as she whipped through Laurel's office door, waving a printout of a spreadsheet. "Stop the presses."

Laurel, headache threatening although the morning had barely begun, glanced up at her assistant. "Why?"

"Well, don't you look grumpy?" Tansy slid the paper onto Laurel's desk. "Maybe this will help."

"Sorry." She pressed a hand to her forehead. "Headache."

"Again? I thought you got rid of him."

Laurel rolled her eyes upward in a warning. "Tansy, don't. Not today."

Two and half weeks without seeing Yates and she still couldn't stop thinking there was more to his sudden cold shoulder than he was saying. Yes, she was pathetic, unable to accept that he simply wasn't that into her.

Worse, the children kept asking about him. Every. Single. Day. Especially Aiden. Yates had called him one final time, apparently with some excuse about the program ending because the kids were moving. The explanation wasn't enough to stop Aiden from missing him.

She missed him too.

"This should cheer you." Tansy patted the spreadsheet. "*Sundown Valley Times* is now operating in the black."

"That is good news."

"Yet you sound as enthusiastic as a politician accepting defeat."

"The kids' aunt comes for them next week."

She'd be alone again. No children. No Yates. Only an ornery grandmother with health issues. Not that she didn't love Gran. She did. But the children and Yates had taught her that she needed more in her personal life. She needed a family of her own.

Now that she'd known the fulfillment they brought, the future without them stretched long and empty in front of her. Like a highway to nowhere.

Prayer brought solace, but the moment she stepped out of her prayer time and into daily life, reality slapped her back down.

She was not one to whine and mope.

But she was definitely moping.

"I'm sorry, Laurel." Tansy perched a narrow hip on the edge of her desk. Her T-shirt proclaimed, *Think like a proton. Stay positive.* Laurel was great at that, except when it came to this situation with Yates. "I know you always wanted kids. Maybe you should sign up for foster care."

"I'm considering it. Except I have trouble letting go."

"Yes, you do. And I'm not talking about the kids. I'm talking about Yates, the guy who hurt you before and now he's done it again. Still, you're moping about as if he matters."

"He's hurting too."

"Stop sympathizing with him. He's the villain."

"He's not. He's struggling with something he can't seem to talk about."

Tansy growled, tossed up her hands and left the office.

With a tired sigh, Laurel opened her desk drawer and took out a bottle of ibuprofen.

Today would be another day of wondering if Tansy and Gran were right, another day of her heart battling her brain. Another day of wondering why.

Most of all, she'd worry about the man she loved.

* * *

Sunday morning, Yates accompanied his family to church. To his surprise, he didn't hate it. He'd even tried praying during the service, but nothing much had happened. Yet instead of rolling his eyes in disbelief, he had listened to Pastor Cloud's message and allowed the ancient words to settle over him.

God had a plan and a purpose for all of us. Getting on God's wavelength, the pastor claimed, made all the difference between living in joy and purpose or struggling through the days, always searching and never finding fulfillment.

Was that where he was? Struggling and searching and coming up short?

The preacher said something else that struck him too.

"According to John 18, there are two kingdoms to choose from," Pastor Cloud said. "The kingdom of God and the kingdom of this world. When you accept Jesus, you step into His kingdom of light. Suddenly, you are governed—not by this world's dark, confused system that changes with the wind but by God's holy, righteous, unchangeable truth. You cannot serve both. The choice is yours. Man's understanding is limited. But God's is infinite. Seek Him. Do what is right in God's eyes, according to His Word."

Do what God says is right.

For a man who'd ignored the Bible for years, Yates wasn't even sure what that meant.

But he aimed to find out.

Anything had to be better than the way he had been living.

Between church, Laurel and the basketball game, he had a lot to think about.

Was God, through his cousin and brother, trying to tell him that his life still had purpose even if he ended up in a wheelchair? That God had a good plan for him?

"Maybe," he mumbled to Justice, who was perched on his haunches between Yates's knees. The dog had found his way into enough sticktights to coat his fur. Patiently, Yates picked and combed the stickers out until he had a pile on the porch floor.

Justice, accustomed to grooming, sat still and waited.

"Next time you explore, pay attention to where you're going."

Justice stared straight ahead as if embarrassed by his misstep.

The sound of children's giggles and conversation floated from the backyard. Justice turned his head the slightest bit.

"I'll let you go back there in a minute," Yates told the dog.

His brother and sister-in-law took advantage of pleasant Sunday afternoons like this one to play outside with the triplets. Justice liked romping with them. Some days Yates enjoyed being with them, too, but today was a day for thinking.

His cell phone buzzed inside his pocket. Without glancing at the caller ID, he dropped the brush to answer.

"Hello."

"Mr. Yates." The childish voice was familiar.

"Aiden?"

"Is it okay if I call you? You said we'd video chat and stuff."

"Sure." Fact was, he felt guilty about the way he'd left things with the boy. In his efforts to set Laurel free, he hoped he hadn't hurt Aiden's feelings. He'd explained that their time was ending anyway, although he could have squeezed in a few more playdates. Except seeing Aiden also meant seeing Laurel, and he couldn't go there.

"What's going on? Everything okay?"

"Aunt Katherine is coming on Tuesday to get us."

"How're you feeling about that?"

"Okay, I guess." He didn't sound too enthusiastic. "I was wondering if maybe we could go fishing one more time before I have to move away. Dad says there's not much fishing in a big city."

The boy's hopeful voice pecked at Yates's conscience. One more fishing trip. One more chance for the boy to enjoy the Kiamichi wilderness.

"Does Laurel know you're calling me?"

"Nah. She's outside in the garden with her granny, so I kinda borrowed her phone. Your picture is right on the front screen, so finding your number was easy. Are you mad at her about something?"

His picture was still on her phone. "No. I'm not mad at her or anybody."

The boy heaved a sigh into the phone. "Good. Will you call her? Ask if I can go fishing? I kinda think she misses you a lot. Gran and her talk sometimes, and I heard her crying in her room."

The stab of guilt was a knife to an open wound. The last thing he'd wanted was to hurt her again. But he had.

Lately he had the wild, irrational thought to tell her about his injuries and forge ahead into a risky future. With her. The selfish part of him wanted to, but was that fair to Laurel?

Until he knew for sure, he'd keep quiet.

But he *could* take this boy fishing one last time.

"I'll call her."

"Can we go today? Right now?"

Jitters hit him in the gut.

"Let me talk to Laurel."

"Okay! I'll take the phone to her. Don't hang up."

"I won't."

While he waited through the sound of running feet and a slamming door, his nerves quivered. He was as anxious as a new recruit on the front line.

Static warned him when the phone changed hands.

"Hello? Yates?" Laurel's sweet voice washed over him.

"Hey." He cleared his throat. "Aiden wants to go fishing this afternoon. You okay with that?"

She hesitated. His heart beat in his ears.

"Did he call you?"

"Yes. But I don't mind. He's leaving soon. I owe him a final outing. Just the two of us."

He'd added the last so she would know he wasn't putting her in the uncomfortable spot of spending time with him.

"Okay. I guess one last fishing trip will be all right. He's really missed you. What time?"

He named the time. "I'll pick him up."

"Fine. Well…"

He wanted to hear more of her voice, but reason said to hang up.

"How are you, Laurel?" he couldn't help asking.

"The paper's doing better. Because of *your* ideas, I think. Jake Trotter said you also had something to do with the increased subscriptions."

Jake Trotter? Good-looking single guy who ran the tire shop?

Was she dating him? "Jake talks too much."

Laurel emitted a small, strained chuckle. "Whatever you did, Yates, thank you."

"No problem. The town needs your paper."

They were talking like strangers, as if they'd never known each other. Yet they both knew too much.

Stiff, uncomfortable, they focused on impersonal conversation while wading through an emotional mire.

Again, the line buzzed with silence.

Finally, Laurel said, "Aiden will be waiting. Thank you for doing this. I know it isn't easy."

"For you either."

"We're big kids. He's not. Bye, Yates."

The receiver clicked. Yates pocketed the phone, cleaned up the pile of sticktights and went to the shed for his fishing equipment.

His ridiculous heart thumped wildly against his rib cage at the notion of seeing Laurel again even for the short moments required to load Aiden and his gear into the truck.

If talking on the phone had turned him upside down, seeing her again might be the end of him.

Laurel paced to the kitchen for a drink of water. Her mouth was as dry as powder.

Yates was on his way.

She glanced down at her blue capris. The knees were dirty from helping Gran in the garden.

She started toward her bedroom to change, then stopped herself. This was not a personal visit. Yates did not care one iota how she looked. He wasn't coming for her. And she had no reason whatsoever to want to impress him.

Grabbing sunscreen and bug spray from the cabinet, she went to find the boy. Aiden had flown into action the moment he heard her agree to the outing. Already, his tackle box and the rod and reel Yates had given him sat by the front door, ready to go.

He came out of the bathroom wearing an army ball cap. Another gift from Yates.

"Sunscreen," she said. "Hold out your arms."

Aiden screwed up his face but stood still while she applied the lotion and then sprayed his pant legs to ward off bugs and ticks.

When she finished, he said, "I'm going to wait outside for Yates."

"He'll be here soon." An unbidden thrill danced over her skin.

The front door slammed, and Aiden's tennis shoes thundered across the porch. Maybe she should remain in the house and simply wave from the doorway.

"Girls," she called down the hallway, "how about some lemonade?"

Two pert faces appeared in the guest room doorway.

"Okay," Chelsey said. "Can we have some pretzels too?"

"Sure. Run see if Gran wants some, okay? I don't want her to overheat."

Chelsey hustled out of the kitchen and quickly returned. "She said yes."

"Great." Though the weather wasn't scorching yet, Gran needed a break from gardening. She tended to overdo it when it came to her flowers. And Laurel needed something to do besides obsess over Yates.

She mixed the lemonade and set out the pretzels, finishing as Gran entered the kitchen, as grimy and sweaty as Laurel had been.

"You all go ahead and snack," Laurel said. "I need to check on Aiden."

Once out on the front porch, she looked around for the boy. "Aiden?"

"I'm up here."

Shading her eyes with one hand, Laurel looked up, following the sound of Aiden's voice. "In the tree again?"

"I'm watching for Yates. I can see way far off from up here."

"You be careful, okay?" Letting Aiden climb the big old oak made her nervous, but when she'd asked his dad, Stephen had assured her that tree climbing was allowed.

"Here he comes. Yates is almost here!" Aiden's voice rose with excitement. "I see his truck!"

He started down from his perch.

"Be careful, Aiden," she said again.

About that time, a big white pickup turned into the

cul-de-sac. She heard the rumble of acceleration. Laurel's heart accelerated too.

Yates.

Laurel swung her attention to the truck and the man inside.

Breath coming annoyingly fast, she wanted to run to him and demand answers to all the questions he'd refused to answer. She wanted to shake him, to kick him in the shins.

To hold him and never let him go.

A snapping noise in the tree above yanked her thoughts toward the oak. She looked up just as the limb gave way.

A cry ripped from her throat.

As if in slow motion, she watched the boy tumble through the air, slamming into branches as he came down from his too-high perch.

And then the awful thud.

Afterward, Yates never remembered how he got from the truck to the boy. Somehow he was on his knees next to Aiden, feeling his pulse, begging him to talk.

He didn't.

"Please, God," Yates whispered. *Don't let anything happen to this sweet boy. For once, hear my prayer. For his sake. Not mine.*

The thought struck him that a fall from such a high place could paralyze the child, especially given how twisted and crooked his body looked.

Paralysis. The word echoed in his brain over and over again.

"Not that, God. I beg you. Not that."

Soon Laurel was kneeling on the opposite side of Aiden, her face white as milk.

Yates's military training kicked in. The same strange,

detached calm he'd felt when an enemy bomb had exploded his body overtook him.

In a quiet voice, he said, "Let's get him to the ER."

"Is he—" She chocked on the question.

"Unconscious. But breathing. Airway is adequate. Pulse is strong. No obvious broken bones. But we're taking no chances."

For a second, his mind flashed back to the day he'd discovered Trent's lifeless body in the bull pen.

He fought off the terrible vision. Aiden was alive. Trent hadn't been.

Supporting the child's neck, he eased Aiden into his arms and ran for the truck, praying all the way, asking for forgiveness, surrendering, aware that God held the reins. Only God. Not him or his expertise. Not his pride or grit or determination. God.

Laurel beat him to the truck and opened the back door. "I'm going with you."

"Get in." Heart nearly pounding out of his chest, Yates jogged toward the driver's side.

"The girls. I should tell Gran."

His tone was curt, in command. "Text her."

The old lady yelled from the front porch. "Go. I've got the girls."

In a roar of powerful engine, Yates started the truck and eased out of the neighborhood. Everything in him wanted to press the gas to the floor and fly, but this wasn't the open countryside. This was a small-town Sunday afternoon with children playing outside.

One disaster today was enough.

Yates hitched his chin toward the back seat. Laurel had crawled in beside the inert child and clung to his little wrist as if willing his pulse to respond. "How's he doing?"

"I wish he would wake up. I'm scared, Yates."

"Me too."

She began to pray.

"Lord in heaven, King of the universe, we need You. Aiden needs You."

"Yes, God," Yates murmured. "Take care of my little buddy."

He choked on the last two words.

"We know that You love us and You care about every single detail of our lives," Laurel prayed, her words trembling from pale lips. "You especially love the little children. I know You're here in this moment and that You've got this child in the palm of your hand. We put our trust in You."

Trust, Yates thought. When had he trusted anyone but himself? And look how that had worked out.

I want to trust You, God. I need to trust Someone bigger and more powerful than me.

The emergency clinic wasn't that far away, but as Yates listened to Laurel pray, an overwhelming peace seemed to enter the vehicle. Did she feel it? Was this God, letting them know that He was here and that He really did hold Aiden in the palm of His hand? That He was worthy of trust?

"God forgive me," Yates whispered as he pulled the truck under the awning of the Sundown Valley Emergency Room.

The clatter of a gurney and the swish of nurses' shoes against shining white-tile floors echoed in Laurel's ears as Aiden was whisked into an exam room.

She couldn't stop shaking.

Yates's arm went around her from the side. "Hey. He's in good hands now."

She couldn't help herself. She leaned into his strength. "I'm so thankful you were there. You knew what to do, and Jesus was in that truck. I felt Him."

Yates nodded, still awed by what he'd felt. "Me too. I've never experienced anything like that *Presence* before."

"Maybe you've been too mad at God to notice."

"Probably. But I can't do it anymore. I'm just so…tired of it. All of it." His deep voice rumbled against her ear. He didn't seem to notice how close they were. Maybe he needed the comfort too.

They could give each other that much.

Through the glass wall, she spotted two tall figures storming across the parking lot like John Wayne and Wyatt Earp.

"Did you call Bowie and Wade?"

"What?" Yates turned toward the entrance. "No." His eyebrows dipped in a frown. "What are they doing here?"

The double glass doors whispered open, and the two cowboys thundered into the waiting room.

Yates went to greet them.

Laurel followed.

"What's going on?" Wade rushed to his brother, eyes dark with fear. "You're standing, in one piece. Are you hurt?"

Wade's eyes traveled over his brother as if expecting the worst.

"Me? No. It's Aiden. He fell."

"Aiden? Okay. That makes sense. I'm glad. Not that he's hurt. But we thought… I thought it was you. That the worst had happened."

Her journalist's intuition began to hum. Yes, she knew he'd been seriously injured in the army, but Wade's anxious words held more than general concern. He was afraid. What did he mean by "the worst had happened"? What was "the worst"?

"I'm fine. But how did you know? What brought you to the hospital?"

Bowie joined the conversation, his calm nature a contrast to Wade's wild intensity.

"We got a garbled, out-of-breath phone call from Laurel's grandmother. She said someone was taken to the ER. We thought it was you." Bowie stopped when he realized Laurel had moved up close to listen.

"Aiden fell from a tree." Grimly, he yanked a thumb toward the exam room. "He's unconscious."

Wade tipped his head back and looked toward the ceiling. "We thought the shrap—"

Bowie elbowed him and shot a pointed look toward Laurel.

Glancing from one cowboy to the other, Laurel narrowed her gaze. What was going on here? Was he about to say "shrapnel"?

Wade yanked off his hat and scrubbed a hand through his hair. "How's the boy?"

"We're still waiting," Laurel said, moving her focus to Yates. "But what's this about your injury?"

Yates glanced away from her probing stare and nodded toward the hallway. "There's the doc now."

They rushed to the ER physician, a large man with a reddish beard and a smiley face name tag.

"How is he?" Yates asked.

"Is he conscious? Will he be all right?"

The doc smiled, though his eyes looked tired. "Yes, he's conscious now but still woozy. We're sending him down for a CAT scan to verify a concussion diagnosis and to be sure there is no other cause for concern. From everything I see and from his general responses, I believe he'll be fine, but I'd like to watch him for a few hours to be sure nothing unexpected pops up."

"No permanent injuries? No broken bones?" Yates asked.

"None that I see at this point. I think he'll recover well in a few days." The doctor smiled again. "As long as he stays out of trees."

Laurel sagged with relief. Yates slipped his arm around

her again and she leaned in. A slight tremor moved through him, letting her know he'd been as anxious as she.

"Can we see him?"

"Soon. When he returns from the scan, you can sit with him until time to take him home."

"I'm so relieved," Laurel said. "Thank you, Doctor."

The physician nodded and hurried toward the next exam room.

"He's going to be okay," she said. "Thank God."

"Yes, thank God," Yates murmured as they walked back to share the good news with the other two men.

"What happened, exactly?" Bowie asked.

"Aiden climbed a tree to watch for Yates."

Yates picked up the story. "I saw the limb snap and Aiden tumble through space. He was out cold. I scooped him up and ran. End of story."

"Wait. Wait. You picked him up?" Wade's look was incredulous. More than that, it was worried. "You aren't supposed to lift anything that heavy."

"Maybe you should have the doc check you out," Bowie said. "Get some X-rays. Just to be sure."

Yates shook his head, his gaze drifting to her. "Let it go, guys."

"Let what go?" she demanded. "I've caught enough innuendo to know there is more to your injury than you've told me. I'm not stupid nor am I a wilting orchid. Someone tell me what's going on."

Both cowboys took a step back, hands raised.

"Not ours to tell," Bowie said and earned a glare from Yates. "Maybe we should go and let you two talk."

Yates growled.

Wade tapped him on the shoulder. "Past time, brother. She's a tough cookie. She can handle it."

"I don't want her to have to."

"Let her decide."

Laurel glared at the three of them. "Would you stop acting as if I can't hear you? Let me decide *what*?" She spun toward the man in question, the man who held her heart in his hands. "Yates, I'm a journalist. We hunt and hound until we get the story. I've suspected all along that something is wrong. Now that I know I was right, I won't let it go. You might as well tell me what they know that I don't."

She watched a battle rage behind the eyes of her beloved. Saw the way he glanced at his family and then at her. Felt his agony of decision.

And she knew the moment he surrendered.

Expression grim, he grumbled, "We need to talk."

Yates gently took Laurel's hand in his and led her to a corner, the most private spot in the waiting room. He wasn't exactly eager to have this conversation, and he sure didn't want the rest of the world to hear.

When he knew they were alone, his brother and cousin standing guard far enough away not to hear but close enough to ward off interruptions, he gathered both of Laurel's hands in his and stared into the eyes of the woman he loved with everything in him.

"I didn't want you to know, Laurel. You matter too much."

"Do I?" The uncertainty in her question broke him.

The day had been too emotional. He struggled to even breathe. He had no energy left to fight. The love in her eyes, in her voice, crumbled him. Over and over again, she'd forgiven him, drawn him back to her.

He dropped his head, wagging it side to side.

"I can't fight them or you anymore. I can't even fight me."

Her hands—those tender, loving hands—slid up his arms. "Sometimes a warrior has to lay down his weapons and let someone else enter the battle. Whatever it is, Yates, let me battle it with you."

His eyes squeezed shut. She was right. He'd been fighting for a long time, the worst battle in the last two years. He was exhausted.

While her gentle hands soothed him like he soothed his horses, he let the story tumble out. When he finished, he glanced up, knowing what he'd see. Love. Acceptance. Strength.

She touched his scruffy jaw. "I love you. I hate that you've gone through such an ordeal and that it still haunts you. But no disability or anything else you may face can change the way I feel, the way I've felt about you for years. Surely, you know that by now."

He did. Just as he'd felt the presence of God in his truck on the drive to the ER, he felt the power of her love all the way through his broken body.

"You shouldn't tie yourself to a man with an uncertain future."

"Oh, Yates, no one knows what the future may hold, but we know Who holds the future. Let's trust Him and each other."

Why she loved him after all he had put her through remained a mystery he didn't want to solve. He only wanted to accept it. His walls tumbled. He had no resistance left.

"I love you so much," he whispered.

"I've waited a long time for you to figure that out."

With a half groan and half laugh, he drew her next to his thunderous heart and hung on for dear life, letting joy and peace and her beautiful, stalwart love wash over him.

Epilogue

Yates squatted in front of his basketball players, giving last-second pointers. The game was on the line, and they had seven seconds left.

"Shane, you take the ball down the court. If the shot's there, take it. If not, quick pass to Jason. Jason, under the rim. Be ready."

The two boys nodded their understanding.

"Becker, block out number six. Keep him out of the box so Shane and Jason can get the last shot." Yates dropped a hand to the shy boy's knee. "You can do it. I've seen that fire in your eyes."

The boy grinned. "We got this, Coach. For you and Miss Laurel."

Only seven seconds left and the score was tied. These boys needed this win. So did he. A victory would be icing on the cake for what he and his team had planned at game's end.

"'Falcons' on three." He stuck his hand in the middle and was met with five much smaller hands along with a feminine one as they broke huddle and spun back onto the court.

Yates glanced at his assistant coach, his heart full. Laurel knew little about basketball rules, but she was a fierce competitor and a wildly encouraging cheerleader. And, to the boys' delight, she brought snacks.

An amazing, nurturing, giving woman. Between her and God, he had no choice but to be happy.

Since the day of Aiden's fall, his life had changed for the better. He'd made up his mind to move forward and let God handle the rest.

He'd intentionally signed on to coach wheelchair kids, was working more on the ranch and, recently, had even ridden a gentle horse. Not far or for long, but he'd been in the saddle without repercussions. He might never train an unbroken mount again, but he was determined to ride.

Life was nothing but chances and choices, and he refused to hide any longer behind the shrapnel in his body.

Most of all, he'd given himself wholeheartedly to the woman standing next to him on the sidelines.

He smiled down at her. She grinned back and pumped her arm. "Go, Falcons!"

The buzzer sounded and play commenced. The clock ticked down.

Six seconds.

Shane drove down court. Number six raced toward him. Becker spun and pivoted, blocking out the other team's main player.

"Good job, Beck! Drive, Shane. Drive."

Three seconds. Shane's eyes flicked toward the clock. Two seconds.

A chant went up from the crowd. *"Shoot. Shoot. Shoot."*

Shane whirled his chair and passed to Jason for the layup.

Yates clenched his fists. His heart thundered. Laurel grabbed his arm and squeezed.

Shoot. Do it. Now.

One second.

The ball went up, circled the rim and, as the crowd

held its collective breath, swished through the net. Noise erupted throughout the gymnasium.

Yates hoisted Laurel into the air. She pounded joyfully on his shoulder, laughing. "We won. Now put me down."

Obediently, he slid her to a stand, grateful that the unthinking outburst hadn't sent pain shooting through his body. He'd healed some, gained weight and almost looked like his old self, but doctors were adamant. He had to be careful. He would never be one hundred percent.

He was learning to be okay with that.

"Huddle up, boys," he called.

Five smiling faces wheeled in unison toward their coach. "We did it, Coach." Shane's giant grin would have won awards.

"Pretty unselfish pass there, Shane," Yates commented.

"We're a team. In this together. You told us that, Coach. I knew Jason would make the shot."

Shane would have, too, but his unselfishness spoke volumes about the boy's character and the character of this team.

Special kids were special for more reasons than their disabilities.

"I'm proud of you. Every single one of you."

With high fives all around, they celebrated the moment.

As the excitement of the win died down, another excitement brewed in Yates's chest. Shane, the team captain, caught his eyes and nodded.

Yates winked, nodding his reply.

All the players, including the substitutes, backed away from the celebration to form a semicircle at center court.

"What are they doing?" Laurel asked.

Yates grabbed her hand. "Come and see."

He glanced up into the stands and waved as his family,

including Bowie's fiancée and her charges, came down the metal steps and gathered at the bottom.

Expression quizzical, Laurel stared at the gathering crowd of friends and family. "What's going on?"

"A celebration." In more ways than one.

"Look. Gran's here," she whispered. "With Tansy."

He knew. He'd invited them. Though Gran still lectured him on a regular basis, she was coming around. And Tansy claimed to know all along that he wasn't the jerk he seemed to be. He took that as a compliment. He even suspected she liked him.

Tugging Laurel's hand, his blood humming, Yates walked her into the half-moon arrangement of players.

Wade released Justice's leash. The dog trotted over to his owner and dropped a small velvet box at his feet.

Yates went to one knee. Justice sat on his haunches at his right side as if in support of this most important mission.

Laurel gasped, touched her lips with shaky fingers. "Yates, what are you doing?"

"Trying to propose, if you'll stop asking reporter questions."

Taking the little jewelers' box from the floor, Yates flipped open the lid. Custom made for her, a large fire opal set in a white-gold twisted-vine design was surrounded by diamonds. More diamonds decorated the figure-eight loops on each side.

"An opal," she breathed. "My favorite. Oh, it's gorgeous."

Never mind the thousands in diamonds. She loved the fiery opal. But he'd known that when he and Bowie, with his artist's eye, helped the jeweler create the design.

"So is it all about the opal, or will you marry me?"

"I'll take both." She laughed, her cheeks rosy and her

eyes glowing. "Oh, I love you so much. You scoundrel. I didn't see this coming. This is perfect."

He slid the ring onto her finger and holding on to her hands, struggled to a stand. He was still off-kilter sometimes, but no one noticed except Laurel, whose grip was strong and sure as he used her for balance.

Pressing those hands to his chest, he said, "I don't have fancy words, and you know I can't promise our life together won't be without challenges. But I can promise that I'll be true and faithful and that I'll love you and put you before me for the rest of our lives."

Expression tender and eyes moist, Laurel stroked gentle fingers across his scruffy jaw. "For better or worse, in sickness and health. I'll mean those vows with all my heart, Yates. The future is for God to decide and whatever it holds, He'll be with us, and we'll be together."

She stood on tiptoe to slide her arms around his neck, face close to his, holding his gaze until his throat filled with emotion. As her lips curved up, he bent to kiss them.

Cheers and applause echoed in his ears. He smiled against her mouth and felt her smile in return.

One kiss didn't seem to be enough, so he bracketed her face in his strong hands and tried another. And another.

"Hey, Coach," Jason's voice interrupted. "Can we go get pizza now?"

A giggle bubbled from Laurel's throat as she pulled away. Blushing and smiling, she was the prettiest woman he'd ever seen.

"Let's go for pizza," she said, "and call the Stafford kids. They'll be excited."

Since the three had moved to Dallas, Yates and Laurel had made two trips and numerous calls. The trio seemed happy in their new home. Aiden had fully recovered, and Stephen was holding his own.

"Sounds like a plan," he said. "Gather your gear, boys, and hit the showers."

As the players rolled toward the locker rooms, Yates and his new fiancée were surrounded by family. His and hers. Trudeaus and Kenos.

No more family feud. No more heartbreaking secrets.

Only love and honesty and openness, no matter what the future might hold.

The prodigal warrior had come home. This time better. This time forever.

* * * * *

Don't miss the first two books in
New York Times *bestselling author Linda Goodnight's*
Sundown Valley series,
To Protect His Children *and* Keeping Them Safe,
available now wherever Love Inspired books are sold!